Melting the Ice . . .

As they waltzed across the floor, he began pulling her into an ever closer embrace. She looked coquettishly away. The little vixen—pretending to be shy! That skin was exquisite, so invitingly smooth. That graceful, long neck, those lips . . . Edmund brought her slowly to a stop. "You really are a beautiful woman," he murmured, and as she blushed he kissed her.

Susan's blush deepened into an angry flush and she pulled back from him. "You must never do that again," she scolded.

Edmund fixed a piercing stare on his dance partner. "At the Blue Boar men and women were more honest about their feelings," he said.

Susan raised her chin to a haughty angle. "May I remind you, sir, that you are no longer an intimate of the Blue Boar? I suggest you adjust your behavior accordingly. The first lady on whom you try that little trick will have you at the altar before the cat can lick her ear."

Edmund slipped his arms around her waist. "And does that apply to you as well, fair Susan?"

Diamond Books by Sheila Rabe

FAINT HEART
THE IMPROPER MISS PRYM
THE LOST HEIR

The Lost Heir

Sheila Rabe

DIAMOND BOOKS, NEW YORK

This book is a Diamond original edition, and has never
been previously published.

THE LOST HEIR

A Diamond Book/published by arrangement with
the author

PRINTING HISTORY
Diamond edition/August 1992

ISBN: 1-55773-758-4

Diamond Books are published by The Berkley Publishing Group,
200 Madison Avenue, New York, New York 10016.
The name "DIAMOND" and its logo are trademarks
belonging to Charter Communications, Inc.

PRINTED IN THE UNITED STATES OF AMERICA

10 9 8 7 6 5 4 3 2 1

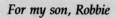

For my son, Robbie

1

"IT IS A lovely night for a robbery," Lady Mary Harriville announced cheerfully to her protégée. Their carriage was traveling at an unnervingly leisurely pace, and the look Miss Susan Montague gave her aunt by marriage did not show her to be amused by this bit of whimsy.

Why they had not put up at an inn long ago was a mystery to Susan. And why two women alone were traveling with no postillions but only a coachman and footman was an equally unanswerable question. Susan had heard many tales of travelers waylaid and robbed, often shot by highwaymen; but she had always assumed that such things couldn't happen to sensible people. And she had always thought her aunt to be a sensible woman. But this freakish behavior, this desire to be out at night, racketing about the countryside when they could have, *should have* put up at that last inn . . . Whatever was Aunt Mary thinking of?

Why the urge to make London tonight?

Susan twisted the strings of the reticule in her lap. It was not up to her to tell her aunt what to do, not with all her aunt was doing for her. Lady Mary had been kind enough to offer to bear the financial burden of a second London season for her niece after the untimely death of Susan's father had cut short her first season. Left with a brood of five daughters ranging from eighteen down to eleven to worry about, Susan's distraught mama had been most grateful. And Susan had been no less grateful than her mother. She owed her aunt a great debt. Nonetheless, she did not like this. "Perhaps we should put up at the next inn we encounter," she suggested timidly.

Lady Mary grimaced, giving herself an extra chin. "Stop? It is early yet," she said.

Her niece politely made no reply to this remark. Earliness, like beauty, seemed to be a subjective thing.

"Besides," Lady Mary added, tucking a stray gray curl back inside her bonnet, "I detest stopping at some of these smaller inns. The sheets are never aired and the poor, unsuspecting traveler is all too likely to find himself sleeping with bedbugs."

"I should rather be contending with bedbugs than highwaymen," said Susan.

Her aunt smiled fondly at her. "Are you afraid, child?"

"I must confess I am feeling increasingly nervous," admitted Susan. "I cannot help recalling what that man at The Swan said."

"Him?" scoffed Lady Mary. "It was certainly in his best interest to pull out as many hobgoblins as he could to frighten us. He had empty rooms to fill." Lady Mary shook her head. "I am sure we will have a dull enough journey," she concluded.

As if on cue, a pistol shot punctuated her sentence. Susan let out a frightened yelp and turned wide eyes on her aunt, who merely shrugged helplessly. "I was wrong," said her ladyship.

Their carriage rolled to a stop and they could hear a male voice barking out orders and the thud of a gun hitting the ground. Both ladies jumped as the carriage door was suddenly yanked open.

A man of unexceptional height, wearing a muffler over his chin and nose, swept off his broad-brimmed hat and made them an elaborate bow. Susan noticed his hair was as unexceptional as his build. It was the color of humus and cut in what looked like a poor man's imitation of the Brutus. But as he stood up two unusual features were quickly discernible in the moonlight: his eyes, which were very blue and showed more intelligence than one would expect to find in such a person; and a birthmark, which ran alongside his temple and splattered onto his forehead. It was not a repulsive mark, for it was not the dark, purplish variety but of a fainter, more reddish color—just the kind of thing one might be teased for as a boy. On a man it was the sort of flaw a new acquaintance would take notice of but forget with friendship. It was also the perfect telltale mark with which to identify a criminal.

Lady Mary had been studying the man as closely as her niece, and now her face lit up with delight. "Edmund!" she declared.

Their captor looked slightly taken aback by this. His eyes widened in surprise, and for a few seconds he looked slightly confused. Susan watched the brows knit and the blue eyes blink. Then the skin around those blue eyes crinkled, as if a broad smile was spreading beneath the dirty muffler. "You must have me confused with another of your acquaintance," he joked, and winked at Susan.

Susan looked affronted and shrunk back against the corner of the coach.

The highwayman's eyes narrowed above his muffler. "I am sorry to interrupt your journey, ladies. But I promise not to detain you long. Would you both be so kind as to step out of the carriage?"

"We certainly shan't," snapped Lady Mary.

Again, the highwayman's eyes widened. A gentle clopping of hooves brought a large man on a dusty black horse into sight. He was holding a pistol casually pointed at the coachman. "Wot's wrong, Dickie boy? Are the ladies givin' you a bit of a problem? That's a new one for you, eh?" He laughed heartily at this. The laugh was swallowed up as suddenly as it had come out and he motioned with his pistol. "Get yer bones out'a the coach," he growled.

Susan jumped and began to comply, but her aunt put out a hand and stopped her. "We are not coming out, but you may come in, Edmund," she informed the first man. "I would have a word with you."

"Aunt!" gasped Susan.

"Edmund!" parroted the large man. "Wot's this Edmund talk?"

"It will be very much worth your while to hear what I have to say," said Lady Mary.

"Don't do it, Dickie boy," cautioned the large man. "The old crow's crazy, she is. And she's probably got a gun hidden in there. She'll blow a hole in your belly the minute you're inside."

"Stubble it," said the highwayman cheerfully. "I always wanted to visit with a fine lady." He climbed inside the coach and shut the door, settling himself on the seat next to Susan who looked anything but pleased to have him next to her. Unoffended, the man chuckled. "Now. What shall we talk about?" he asked.

"Your future," said Lady Mary.

The highwayman squirmed. "You ain't one of those crazy people who go around asking about others' souls, are you?" he asked warily.

"No," said Lady Mary. "Though God knows, it wouldn't have hurt you if I were. Tell me, young man, where are your people? Do you have parents?"

"Everyone has parents," replied the highwayman evasively.

"And yours, do they know their son earns his bread and butter by riding up and down the king's highway, terrifying innocent travelers out of their possessions?"

"I don't see as how that's any of your business," snapped the young man.

Lady Mary seemed unoffended by his rudeness,

but sat staring at him, contemplating. "Do you enjoy being a highwayman?" she asked at last.

"Of course I enjoy being a highwayman," said the man, irritated.

"How would you like to get ahold of a fortune large enough to enable you to live the rest of your life in ease and comfort?"

The highwayman looked from Lady Mary to her niece, and the expression in his eyes plainly showed he thought them both insane.

"You'll never have to worry about ending your days swinging on Tyburn Hill," said Lady Mary.

"Who says I will wind up there, anyway?" countered the highwayman.

"Any young man foolish enough to stop a coach in full moonlight and display such a telling mark as the one you bear on your temple is bound to end on Tyburn Hill," said her ladyship.

Sudden fear showed in the young man's eyes and he reflexively pulled his hat lower over his face.

"It is too late for that, my fine friend," continued her ladyship ruthlessly. "For both my niece and I have seen that mark. Of course," she said casually, "you could silence us, but I don't think you are a heartless killer. Would you kill an old woman and an innocent girl?"

"I would if I had to," blustered the highwayman. "So you'd best remember that and keep your gabblebox shut. Both of you," he added, giving Susan a menacing look.

Susan's face paled, and she nodded and suggested to her aunt in a weak voice that perhaps the gentleman would like to be on his way. "If we just give him our jewels, then we can be going, too, and we will simply forget this incident ever happened. I am sure I never liked this necklace by half." She put her hands to her neck.

"Leave your necklace where it is," commanded Lady Mary. "Now, young man. Where were we? Ah yes, Tyburn Hill. You will surely end up there, you know. Or, rather, you would have if we had not come along. Pull down your muffler."

"What!" The highwayman was incensed.

Lady Mary whacked him on the leg with her cane. "Do as you are bid."

The highwayman was shocked into complying.

"Now pull off your hat," continued Lady Mary. The hat came off, and she and the highwayman sat regarding each other, Lady Mary's look highly contemplative, the man's wary. "So," she said at last. "Should you like to live the life of wealth I described?"

"Who would not?" answered the highwayman. "And just what do I have to do to get this life, kill off some nob for you?"

Lady Mary's face registered disgust. "Really! I can see we will have much work to do on you."

"On me?" Again, the highwayman began to squirm. "Just what the devil is it you want me to do?" he asked uneasily.

"Nothing to which you are not equal, I assure you," said her ladyship. "All you need to do is prove you are the Duke of Grayborough."

2

THE HIGHWAYMAN BEGAN to laugh. "Oh, that's rich," he chortled. "Me, a duke."

Susan saw no humor in Lady Mary's remark. "Aunt Mary, you cannot be serious," she protested.

"I have never been more serious in my life," replied her aunt. "What is your name, young man?"

The highwayman wiped his eyes. "Richard White," he said. "But you can call me Your Lordship," he added, and broke into fresh laughter.

"The proper way to address a duke is 'Your Grace,' " corrected Lady Mary.

The carriage door swung open and the big man stuck his head inside. "Wot's goin' on in here?" he demanded. "Are you goin' to rob these nobs or have a bloody tea party with 'em?"

"Don't talk to me like that," said the highwayman. He pinched his nose and raised his chin and said, "I'm a duke."

"Oh, and I'm the Prince Regent," said his friend. "Come on, Dickie boy. Let's be done." He indicated Lady Mary with a jerk of the head. "This one's a queer one, no doubt about it. And the sooner we're gone from here the better I'll like it."

"He's not going with you, so you may shut the door and leave," said her ladyship.

"Wot!" bellowed the large man. "Now look here, you old, er . . ." Lady Mary's outraged stare made his sentence crumble.

"Shut the door and wait," ordered his friend. "The duchess and I ain't done having our chat." The large man frowned but obeyed, and the highwayman turned his gaze back on Lady Mary.

"Mr. White, eh?" she said, picking up the threads of their lost conversation. "How did you acquire that name?"

The highwayman's smile faded. "What's wrong with my name?" he asked.

"Nothing is wrong with your name," replied her ladyship. "It is a good, honest name, and that is better than we can say of the fellow who bears it. Who gave it to you?"

"Old Jonsey's wife, Mrs. Jones—Mother to me. She's all the mother I ever had. And there was none better in all of England," the man added, as if daring either of the women with him to say a word against Mrs. Jones.

"Why did they not call you Richard Jones?" asked Lady Mary.

The highwayman shrugged. "I suppose 'tis because no one knew what to do with me when

I first showed up at the Blue Boar."

"The Blue Boar?" repeated Susan faintly.

"There's no finer place to get good stout in all of Sussex," insisted the highwayman.

"I am sure there is not," agreed Lady Mary. "Please continue with your story."

The highwayman shrugged. "Little else to tell. No one showed up to claim me. They had to call me something. So they called me Richard—Dick, after the Jones's first son what died as a baby. And they named me White 'cause they said I looked white as a sheet when I first entered the inn."

"How old were you when they found you?" asked Lady Mary.

The highwayman shrugged again. "Can't remember," he said.

"Well, you shan't be Richard White any longer," said her ladyship firmly. "From now on you are Edmund Morris Worthington, rightful Duke of Grayborough. We shall prove your claim and supplant the present duke."

"Whoa," said the man, holding up a hand. "There is already a duke?"

"There is one who holds the title who has no right to it," said Lady Mary.

"Aunt Mary," protested Susan. "The Duke had every right to the title. He was next in line."

"Edmund had the right to that title," declared Lady Mary. "Not Jonathan. For years he has enjoyed something that is not his to enjoy, and I intend to put an end to it." Susan looked shocked by this speech and her aunt waggled a finger at her and said, "I know what you are thinking. You are thinking I am a spiteful old woman out to put a spoke in my cousin's wheel. Well, if ever a wheel deserved a spoke it is Jonathan's, the wicked old miser."

The highwayman was totally at sea in this conversation, and he found himself wishing he had stayed comfortably ensconced in his warm corner table at The Swan and never ventured out this night. The old crow had seemed such a rich, easy bird for the plucking. Richard had always been one to rise to a challenge and hearing the old woman proclaim her lack of fear had been a challenge he couldn't resist. Two rich women and no protection. It had seemed too good to be true. That'll teach you, Dickie boy, to go chasin' after things what seem too good to be true. It's 'cause they are, he thought. The old crow was dicked in the noodle and he wanted nothing more than to get away. "Well, it has been an interesting night, ladies," he said. "But I really ought to be on my way. Old Samson is probably getting itchy to be gone." He reached for the door and had his arm soundly rapped by her ladyship's cane.

"I would tell you a story," she said.

"Oh, gawd," moaned the highwayman, and was rapped again.

"Don't be impertinent," snapped Lady Mary. "And please keep in mind that you are in the presence of ladies and watch your tongue."

The highwayman threw himself against the squabs of the coach, crossed his arms over his chest, and scowled. But he remained.

"Fifteen years ago," said Lady Mary, "my family experienced a great tragedy. It was not our first, but it was certainly our greatest. My brother, the Duke, was crippled. He became so after a carriage accident that took the life of his wife. This was a great blow to my brother, but he was a man of sanguine temperament." She nodded at the highwayman. "Much like you. And though he grieved over his loss, he tried to make the best of things. He had two fine sons and many friends, and in spite of his weak health he lived a full life, giving generously to those in need, entertaining frequently." Lady Mary gazed at some invisible scene. "He loved his fellow men, my brother did. He was very fond of cards and often held card parties. The footmen would carry him downstairs and he would preside over the party just as if he were a whole man." Lady Mary blinked and wiped her eyes. "And house parties, he was very fond of house parties. It was at a house party that the tragedy struck.

"My husband was still alive at the time, and he and I were present, as well as my cousin Jonathan, who is the current Duke, and his wife and son Jarvis. My nephews wanted to take their cousin Jarvis and go shoot pheasant, but my brother felt them too young to go alone—Gerard was twelve, Edmund and Jarvis only nine—so, Jonathan offered to take the boys. The morning of the accident Jonathan, Gerard, and young Edmund went into the copse. Young Jarvis had come down with a nasty cold in the night and did not go. Three went out that morning. Only one returned."

"What?" The highwayman sat up. "What are you saying?"

"Gerard, the future Duke of Grayborough, was shot and killed. Jonathan said he was sure it was an accident. The boy shot—"

"No!" interrupted the highwayman. "Say no more. I wish to hear no more of this sorry tale."

"You must hear it," said Lady Mary. "Edmund accidentally shot and killed his brother. Shocked by what he had done, he ran away. Jonathan carried Gerard back to the house and the doctor was summoned. Servants were sent to find Edmund but returned without him. Jonathan and my husband joined in the search as well but came back equally unsuccessful. The boy was never found. The shock of all this was too much for my brother. He died within a week of his eldest son."

A long silence fell in the carriage. At last the highwayman broke it. "And you want me to be this Edmund fellow, the one what killed his brother? Faugh," he finished in disgust. "I ain't going to masquerade as no bloody killer."

"Edmund was not a killer," snapped Lady Mary. "A sweeter, kinder boy you would not find. And he adored his older brother. No one thought to blame the boy for Gerard's death. We would have all done our best to help him through the difficult time that lay ahead. All of us except my cousin Jonathan, that is. He was the one who pushed to have the boy finally declared dead. 'There is no sense in waiting forever,' he said."

"He waited ten years," put in Susan timidly. "It does seem a long time—"

"Ha!" snorted Lady Mary. "If Jonathan could have found a way he would have been Duke of Grayborough within a month. He couldn't wait to step into his little cousin's shoes. And now I cannot wait to take him out of them."

The look Lady Mary gave the highwayman was half pleading, half challenging. "You are Edmund," she said. "I had only to see your face to know it. The title does not belong to my cousin. Only you can take it from him."

"I ain't Edmund!" declared the young man hotly. "I'm Dick White. I'm a bloody highwayman, and I like who I am and don't want to be some nob what killed his brother. I won't do it!"

"If you don't do it, you'll be gallows meat for sure," said Lady Mary. "Have you ever seen a man hanged to death? It is not a pretty sight, I assure you. And it must be a most painful way to die, to feel that band of rope burning your flesh, cutting off your air . . ."

The highwayman's hand slipped up and pulled at the neck of his shirt.

"On the other hand," continued Lady Mary sunnily, "you may become Grayborough and right an old wrong. You will live a life of ease, have all the money and playthings you like—fancy carriages and horses, gambling money, elegant clothes. Pretty ladies will set their caps for you . . ."

The man who called himself Richard White chewed his lip in contemplation and regarded the young woman sitting next to him. She had hair the color of chestnuts, large eyes, and a long, graceful neck. Around that neck fell a string of tiny pearls. A duke had blunt enough to buy a basketful of such geegaws. And a man with that much blunt could also buy himself a fine woman, not some cheap trollop. The young woman blushed under his speculative gaze and the highwayman grinned and winked at her. Nodding in her direction he asked the older woman, "Will we be related?"

"Only by marriage," replied her ladyship, a sudden twinkle in her eyes.

The highwayman resumed chewing his lip. It would be fun to be a duke for a while. If he didn't like it he could always bolt. "All right," he said with a cheerful slap of the thigh. "I'll do it."

Susan was visibly upset. She turned to her aunt. "How can you possibly expect to pass such a man off as nobility?"

Lady Mary shrugged. "His manners are little worse than some of the young rakes I have seen lounging about town. Besides, manners are easily learned. In the end it is breeding that counts." Before her niece could object to this illogical reasoning, Lady Mary leaned her head out the window. "Jameson," she called.

A disembodied voice floated to them from outside the carriage. "Yes, Your Ladyship?"

"Come down here, please."

"Your Ladyship," began the doubtful reply.

"Oh, yes. Your friend," said Lady Mary. "Will you please be so good as to rid us of his unnecessary presence?"

The new Edmund turned to Susan and held out his hand. "The necklace," he said.

Susan's chin went up.

"I have to give him something," said the highwayman. "If I am a duke now I can afford to buy you another."

"Aunt Mary!" protested the girl, but Lady Mary merely nodded her agreement with her new nephew, and Susan ungraciously complied, giving the highwayman a look of disgust along with the necklace.

He leaned out the window and summoned his friend. He tossed the necklace to him. "Here, old giant. This ought to buy a few rounds at the Blue Boar."

The large man caught the necklace, held it up and examined it. " 'Tis a beauty," he announced. "What else?"

"That is all you get," laughed the new Edmund. "Now run along home and tell old Jonsey he won't be seeing me any more."

"Wot?" demanded the large man. "Wot do you mean by that?"

"I mean, I am going with the ladies. 'Tis my lucky day, old fellow. I am going off to try my hand at being a duke."

"A duke?" echoed the large man. "What the devil are you gabblin' about? You ain't no gentry cove."

"This lady wants to pass me off as a duke, and I am going to let her try."

"A duke? Why you?"

"Because I talk better than you."

"Oh, you're balmy," scoffed the other man.

"Maybe," agreed Edmund. "But that is what I am going to do, so you trot along, and I'll write and let you know what being a duke is like."

"You know I can't read," objected his friend.

"Then I'll come and visit you," promised Edmund. "Now, go on will you?"

"Well," said the large man doubtfully. "If you're sure."

"I am."

The big man smiled sadly at him. "I'll miss you, Dickie boy, you little half-pint. If you ever get lonely you know where to find some good company."

"Aye," said Edmund. "Now go on, you big oaf. Go find Mary and give her a kiss for me."

The large man brightened. "I'll be glad enough to do that," he said, and with a whoop he spurred his horse and galloped away.

Susan let out a sigh and collapsed against the squabs, and Lady Mary again called to her coachman. Jameson's head appeared at the window. "Are you all right?" she asked.

"They winged John," said the driver, venturing a hateful look inside the coach.

Lady Mary frowned and Edmund shrugged apologetically. "But we never shoot to kill," he said.

"I should hope not," said Lady Mary. "We will proceed home now," she informed her coachman.

The man's jaw dropped. "Begging Your Ladyship's pardon, but what about—" he began.

"His grace will be proceeding home with us," said Lady Mary calmly.

The coachman's eyes popped and he stood rooted to the ground.

"Don't stand there gaping, Jameson. Do as I bid you," she commanded.

The coachman did as he was told, shaking his head and muttering about the peculiarities of the upper classes. Within minutes Lady Mary Harriville was conveying the future Duke of Grayborough to London.

The party finally arrived at Lady Mary's London townhouse in the wee hours of the morning. The servants had been sent on ahead to ready the house for her and everyone had, indeed, been ready but not for the unusual house guest she had brought with her. In spite of his years of training, her butler could not conceal his surprise and distaste at the sight of Edmund.

"Harris, this is my long-lost nephew, Edmund," said Lady Mary.

Edmund recalled himself from taking in his grand surroundings and held out his hand. "How d'ye do?" he said.

Harris stared at the hand as if it were leprous.

"Edmund," corrected Lady Mary. "It is not proper to shake hands with the servants."

Edmund flushed and mumbled an apology.

"Never mind," said his aunt kindly. "You will learn in time. We shall put Edmund in the earl's old bedroom," she told the butler. "Please see him up."

"Very good, Your Ladyship," said Harris. "If Your Grace would care to follow me?"

"I guess that's me, huh?" joked Edmund nervously.

Lady Mary smiled and patted his arm. "You

will do fine in your new life," she assured him. Again, she turned to Harris. "We shall have to find a valet for His Grace. For tonight you may send James to him."

"Well, goodnight, Your Ladyship," said Edmund.

Lady Mary smiled at her new nephew. "To the servants I am Your Ladyship, Edmund. To you I am Aunt."

Edmund returned the smile. "Yes, Aunt," he said and followed Harris upstairs.

An exhausted looking Susan fell in behind him with Lady Mary bringing up the rear.

Once in her room, Susan gave herself up to the ministrations of her abigail who had been anxiously awaiting her arrival. "We thought your carriage was following not more than an hour behind us," said the girl, rushing to help her mistress out of her gown. "I was getting that worried about you, Miss."

"We were right behind you . . . until Aunt decided to stop at that inn." Susan rubbed her tired head.

"Well, you're here now, and we'll have you in bed in no time," said the little maid comfortingly.

Yes, bed. That was what she needed. All thoughts of her aunt's eccentricities were left behind as Susan contemplated the pleasure of tumbling into a bed welcomingly warmed with hot bricks.

Edmund eyed the large, curtained bed in his room with equal pleasure. The butler pulled a cord hanging by it and launched into a stiff speech welcoming His Grace back and telling him if he needed anything he had only to ring. . . .

"That's very nice, thank you," said Edmund. "All I need is to shut my peepers for a while and I'll be fine." He plopped onto the bed and began to pull off his boot.

"If Your Grace would care to wait, I have rung for James," said the butler.

"Rung for James? What do you mean by that?" asked Edmund, boot in hand.

"I mean, Your Grace, that he will be here any minute."

Edmund scowled and tossed his boot on the floor. He yanked off the other. All he wanted to do was sleep. Now this Harris fellow was inviting people up to his room. He supposed it must be because the man wanted him to feel welcome in his new home. But that could all wait till he'd had a decent sleep. "Look here, old fellow," he said, rising to clap a startled Harris on the back. "It was very nice of you to want to get a little welcoming party going, but I'm bloody fagged, and all I want to do is sleep."

"I understand, Your Grace," said Harris patiently. "And we shall endeavor to assist you to that end with all possible speed."

"What?" said Edmund.

There was a knock at the door and Harris and Edmund called out at the same time, "Come in," and "Go away." Looking like a severely tried saint, Harris opened the door. Another man entered. He was tall and wore a powdered wig and blue satin. "His Grace would like to get ready for bed," said Harris. "Until we can secure a valet for him her ladyship wishes you to assist him."

The man in the fancy clothes looked at Harris as if he suspected a joke. "She was completely in earnest, I assure you," the butler said and left the room.

With a grim smile the man approached Edmund. "Allow me, Your Grace," he said, and laid hold of Edmund's coat.

No man ever took Richard White by surprise. He swung around and punched the man in satin in the eye.

The footman's hand flew to his face and he staggered back into the dressing table, knocking bottles and brushes from it, and finally tipping both himself and the table onto the floor.

Edmund's door opened and the butler rushed in. "Your Grace," he gasped. "James!"

"He hit me," announced James, staggering to his feet. "I went to take his coat and he hit me."

"This fellow tried to jump me!" bellowed Edmund.

"Oh, heavens!" exclaimed Susan from the doorway. She was clad in a wrapper, her hair falling in loose curls about her shoulders. Edmund temporarily forgot the footman as he imagined how those chestnut curls would look spread out over a pillow. "I shall fetch Aunt," she said.

But Lady Mary had been right behind her. She brushed past her niece into the room. "What is going on here?" she demanded.

"This fellow attacked me," said Edmund.

"Your Ladyship, I only tried to assist him with his coat," protested poor James.

"So you say," scoffed Edmund. He turned to Lady Mary. "The minute that Harris fellow was gone he tried to jump me. Help with my coat. Ha! Why the devil would I need help taking off my coat? I've been doing it by myself for years," he concluded in disgust.

"The nobility do not dress themselves," said Lady Mary severely.

"Lord love you," said Edmund in awe. "I heard such a thing once, but I thought the fellow what was telling me was bamming me."

Her Ladyship sighed in exasperation and turned to her wounded footman. "I am sorry this happened. You may be sure I will compensate you for the discomfort my nephew unknowingly inflicted on you."

"Thank you, Your Ladyship," murmured James.

"Your services will not be required tonight," said Her Ladyship. "Go down to the kitchen and put a steak on that eye." To her new nephew she said, "Just for tonight I shall allow you to prepare for bed alone. Now, let us all see if we can get some sleep." She left the room with Susan in her wake.

This sounded fine to Edmund, and as soon as his door shut he heaved himself out of his coat and fell into bed, still wearing his breeches and shirt.

Susan soon found her bed as well, and in it a deep and dreamless slumber. She awoke late the next morning to wonder to her maid if she had, perhaps, dreamed the previous night's adventures. Had those strange doings taken place only behind closed eyelids?

The summons to her aunt's bedroom led her to suspect it had not. And her aunt's words to her confirmed those suspicions. "Susan, love, I have come to the conclusion that turning Edmund into a duke is going to be a Herculean undertaking."

Susan sighed. "Then I did not dream all the things that happened last night," she murmured.

Her aunt chuckled. "No. I am afraid you did not."

"Aunt Mary, why are you doing this?" asked Susan earnestly.

"Because it must be done," said her ladyship simply. "I always thought there was something havey-cavey about the way Edmund disappeared when Gerard was killed," she mused. "I don't know what Jonathan said to the boy to make him run away, but I am sure he said something."

"But surely this whole plan is equally havey-cavey," said Susan.

"He is Grayborough," said Lady Mary calmly. Her niece stared at her as if something in her aunt's brain had come unhinged and Lady Mary smiled at her. It was the tolerant smile one would give to an exceptionally stupid yet greatly-loved child. "I am, of course, sorry this has coincided with your season."

Susan waved this comment aside. "Surely you don't think something so petty as concern for a London season prompted me to speak," she said.

"No, child. I know you better than that. You are a good girl, kind and generous. Which is why I have no qualms in asking you what I am about to ask."

3

SUSAN SANK INTO a nearby chair, a look of dread on her face.

"Now, my dear, please do not look as if I am about to feed you to a dragon," said Lady Mary. "I merely wish you to help me instruct Edmund in how to get on in polite society."

Susan sat silent, obviously struggling with a variety of warring emotions.

"I know it is asking a great deal," said Lady Mary humbly. "It is terrible of me to use you so, and I suspect if you did not feel obliged to help you would instantly decline."

Susan blushed at her aunt's perspicacity. "It is true," she admitted. "Ungrateful wretch that I am, I would rather face wild tigers than try and tame this person. But I am fully aware of the debt I owe you."

"I am not asking you to pay a debt, my dear, for you owe me none. If you would rather not be involved I shall undertake this alone."

"No," said Susan firmly. The new Edmund was too large a handful for any one person. "I shall help you."

"Thank you," said Lady Mary. "You are doing my family a great service."

"I hope they may think so," said Susan doubtfully.

She was still harboring doubts when Edmund joined the ladies for a late breakfast. Although he did have a charming smile, his table manners were atrocious. Susan tried not to watch him eat, but like a bird hypnotized by a snake, she found herself unable to keep her eyes from him.

He smiled at her. " 'Tis a shame you pinned up your hair," he said. "It looked beautiful last night." Susan blushed and his smile widened. "I don't see why women do all those silly things to their hair, anyway," he complained. "I'd wager most men would as soon see a woman with her hair down. There's nothing like the feel of soft curls under a man's fingers, unless, of course, it's soft. . . ."

"Edmund!" snapped Lady Mary.

Edmund jumped. He looked from Susan, whose face was apple red, to his aunt, who was frowning disapprovingly, and shut his mouth.

"It is no more proper for a man to talk of such things in the presence of a young lady than it is for a woman to go 'round with her hair unpinned," said Lady Mary.

"The nobs are a stuffy lot," muttered Edmund.

"You will find many members of the nobility

to be anything but stuffy," said Lady Mary. "I am sure you will find a great number of young rakehells with whom you may curse and gamble and behave abominably. And I am sure such a comment as you have just made would not be offensive to an older, married female bent on dalliance. God knows we have enough of them."

"Do we?" asked Edmund, brightening.

"But," continued Lady Mary, ignoring this remark, "a young, innocent female is expected to remain so. And a gentleman is expected to do all that is in his power to help her."

"I will only talk to the married ones," said Edmund. "It sounds simpler."

His aunt smiled at this. "Don't be ridiculous," she said. "Even if you wished to do so, you could not avoid the younger ones. Every matchmaking mama in London will be throwing her daughter at you once your claim is proved. After all, you will be the Duke of Grayborough. You will be wealthy and titled. Even if you were not a passably nice-looking young man, those two things alone would assure you of being pursued by a bevy of young ladies."

Edmund had rarely lacked for feminine attention, and it was comforting to know that this happy circumstance would continue. He eyed Susan, who squirmed uncomfortably under his gaze. He would definitely like to add her to his collection of fair admirers.

Susan was anything but an admirer of Edmund's. "Whoever will believe such a person to be Edmund Worthington?" she asked her aunt later as they sat waiting for him to return from his first shopping expedition.

"Wait and see, child," said Lady Mary. "I will grant you, he is a rogue and a scoundrel now. But he has charm. And a good heart. I am confident he will polish up well. New clothes will help, too."

"I never subscribed to Mr. Brummel's theory that clothes make the man," said Susan.

"New clothes may not be the making of him, but Edmund's old ones certainly would have been the breaking of him," said Lady Mary. "I am sure that between the two of them, Harris and James will be able to give him some proper guidance in that area."

Susan giggled at the mention of her aunt's trusty servants. "Poor Harris. He thought he was to have the afternoon off."

Her aunt smiled. "I shall give him the evening off," she said. "He will most likely need it."

"And James," continued Susan. "Did you see his face when you told him he was needed to help Edmund choose a wardrobe?"

"I think he bears my nephew a grudge," sighed Lady Mary.

"How small of him," teased Susan. "His eye is not so very black, after all. Oh, Aunt," she said, suddenly serious. "I am not at all sure about the wisdom of what we are doing."

"What I am doing, don't you mean?" corrected Lady Mary. Susan blushed and her aunt chuckled. "It was most polite of you to include yourself in my folly. I must admit our Edmund is proving to be a handful. I suppose we had best keep him out of sight tomorrow. He is not yet ready to be turned loose on society."

But Edmund had no desire to be kept out of sight when he heard the next morning that his aunt was having company. He wanted to show off his new clothes. "Stay in my room!" he cried. "But, why?"

"You will be more comfortable there," said her ladyship politely.

"The devil I would," objected Edmund.

"We will be receiving afternoon calls today and will have many ladies coming and going, and, as you are not yet ready to make your social debut—"

"I am, too, ready," insisted Edmund. "I have new clothes."

"That does not make you ready for polite company," said his aunt. "I think this would be easiest."

Edmund frowned. "How long am I to stay cooped up, anyway?"

"Only until the ladies have gone."

"And how long will that be?"

"Not so very long. You may come out in time for dinner."

"Dinner! You mean I am to stay in my room the whole bloody afternoon?"

"I think it would be best," said her ladyship. "James will attend you. He will provide you with anything you desire."

"A wench," cracked Edmund.

"This," said his aunt frostily, "is why you are not ready for polite society. You may, of course, have any books, wine or brandy—"

"Faugh," spat Edmund. "How I ever let myself get talked into this duke nonsense I'll never know. A duke my foot. I ain't nothing but a bloody prisoner."

"As you are only being asked to remain in your room for one afternoon," said her ladyship, "I am sure it is a hardship that you will be able to endure."

Banished to his room, Edmund, like Cain, found his punishment more than he could bear. He began to pace. "I never thought I'd live to see the day I'd have females running my life, telling me what to do, what to say, locking me in my room!" His voice grew to a roar and he gave his bellpull a vicious jerk.

Harris appeared. "Yes, Your Grace?"

"Send James to me," Edmund commanded. "Tell him to bring two bottles of port and a deck of cards."

"Yes, Your Grace," murmured Harris and vanished.

"Yes, Your Grace," mimicked Edmund and kicked over a chair. I could leave, he thought suddenly. But with that thought came the memory of the previous day's shopping expedition. The old girl had spent a lot of blunt outfitting him. Well, she could take the bloody clothes back and tell those shopkeepers she didn't want 'em. He was damned if he was going to hang around and let a couple of females run his life.

His ranting thoughts slowed. One of those females had curst pretty hair. And a fine figure.

And she liked him, he was sure of it. Of course, she wouldn't admit it yet, not even to herself, but she liked him. He could tell.

Well, he'd stay for a few days. Enjoy his new togs, see the city. Then he'd be gone. And why not? After all, the old lady had as good as lied to him. Dukes didn't live such a wonderful life. They had somebody telling them what they could and couldn't do every time they turned around. A fellow couldn't even get dressed by himself! "I'll just stay awhile," Edmund repeated out loud, and suddenly a vision of Tommy Smith, the Blue Boar's resident drunkard, reaching for his glass and saying "I'll just have one more" came to mind. "Oh, no, Dickie boy. You're not like that," Edmund assured himself.

James's arrival with cards and wine ended Edmund's conversation with himself. "Well, James," he said heartily. "I hope you are good at cards. And why have you brought only one glass?"

The footman's eyes widened. "Your Grace, I cannot—" he began.

"You cannot sit here and watch me drink alone," Edmund finished for him. "That is true. Well, never mind. You can have the glass. I will drink from the bottle." He flopped onto the floor and motioned for James to join him. James hesitated. "My good fellow, did not my aunt instruct you to see to my needs today?" asked Edmund.

James nodded. "Well, I am in need of company. So please come and plant your bones and let us get started."

James nervously complied, and an hour later he

was pounding the floor and laughing uproariously with Edmund over a ribald joke. Two hours later he was stretched out on the floor, snoring.

Edmund shook his head. "Fellow can't hold his wine," he said. He brushed a speck of lint from his new shirt and yawned. What to do now? Solitaire? No. Edmund was lonely. He got up and put on his old coat. Its cheapness, both in cloth and cut, contrasted irritatingly with his new pantaloons and shirt, but he suspected his aunt would rather he wore his old coat than no coat at all. "Pity that Weston fellow didn't have something on hand that fit," he muttered as he sauntered out of his room.

Downstairs, Lady Mary was presiding over a gathering of half a dozen ladies. Once she and her guests had heard the distant rumble of male laughter and a thumping noise as if someone was banging on the floor. But they had all politely ignored it. Susan had glanced worriedly at her aunt, who merely smiled at her and asked her if she would care for another cup of tea.

The high-pitched shriek of one of Lady Mary's maids followed by a rich male laugh coming from the hall outside the drawing room door, however, was not so easily ignored.

Nor was the man who entered the room. It wasn't his height or broad chest that caught the ladies' attention, for he had neither. But he had a fine, trim figure, lovely blue eyes, and a deeply dimpled smile. The birthmark on his face prevented him from being handsome, but there was something so very male about him that the young ladies squirmed, nervous with their instinctual reactions, and the older ones smiled.

Of course, if Edmund himself wasn't enough to attract attention, his dress certainly was. A good deal of his attire bespoke the gentleman. His buff-colored pantaloons were obviously new and made of the finest merino cloth. His shirt, too, was most elegant. But the coat was nothing any gentleman of the haut ton would be caught near, let alone in. Its worn-looking, stained cloth proclaimed that it had seen better days long ago.

Susan clamped her lips together in exasperation.

Edmund sauntered into the room, the picture of confidence, and ogled a pretty young lady, who blushed to the roots of her hair and quickly lowered her gaze.

"Edmund!" said her ladyship sharply. Edmund jumped and Lady Mary politely asked him to be seated. He grinned at her as if he had won a victory and seated himself next to her on the settee. "This is my nephew, Edmund Morris Worthington, the lost Grayborough heir," she announced.

There were cries of surprise and a gentle rustling of whispers. Under the hubbub Lady Mary turned, smiling, to her nephew and hissed, "What are you doing here?"

"I got bored," he answered.

Lady Mary gave an exasperated sigh. "Don't say anything," she commanded. "Smile and nod and let me speak."

Edmund smiled and nodded.

"But everyone thought you were dead," protested one lady.

"Oh, I suppose I might have been if I'd kept on the way I was going," said Edmund cheerfully.

"Have a biscuit, Edmund," said his aunt in threatening tones.

Edmund looked properly reproved and took a biscuit. Susan glared at him and he shrugged defensively.

"I am sure your family is glad to find you after all these years," said another woman.

"Yes, well, Edmund has just newly come to stay with us," said Lady Mary.

"Has the duke, er, I mean . . ."

"My cousin is not yet aware of our family's great good fortune," said Lady Mary.

Edmund had been eyeing a pretty little thing with dark curls and lashes. "And who might this be?" he asked.

"This is Miss Ravenscort," said his aunt. "And this—"

"Ravenscort, eh?" interrupted Edmund, leering at the girl. "You can perch on my window sill any time, little bird."

The nostrils of the plump woman sitting next to the girl flared and her eyebrows disappeared somewhere under her turban.

"And this is Baroness Ravenscort," finished her ladyship between clenched teeth. "Miss Ravenscort's *mama.*"

"There is no need to tell me that," said Edmund, recovering his footing. "I can see where the child gets her beauty. Baroness, I am heartily glad I did not meet you when you was a young girl. You would have broken my heart, I am sure."

Did Edmund really think he could repair the damage he'd done with such outrageous flattery? Lady Mary and Susan both watched.

To their amazement, the corners of Baroness Ravenscort's downturned mouth lifted. Edmund continued to flatter her and she preened and simpered, and by the time she was ready to take her leave Edmund had been transformed into a dear boy; a poor, long-suffering, dear boy.

The last caller finally left and the ladies breathed a sigh of relief. "Bolt the door, Harris," said Lady Mary. "We are no longer at home to anyone." She fixed a hard stare on Edmund.

"I got tired of being stuck alone in my room."

"James was with you," pointed out his aunt.

"Er, yes," said Edmund, thinking of the footman snoring blissfully in his room. "You may need to give him the evening off."

Lady Mary's brows shot up. "And why might I need to do that?"

"He probably will not be feeling too wonderful when he wakes up."

"When he wakes up?" repeated Lady Mary. "Oh, Edmund! What have you done?"

Edmund crossed his legs and tried to appear nonchalant. "We just got to playing piquet and drinking port, and I suppose poor old James don't have much of a head for the stuff," he finished apologetically.

"Edmund, Edmund." Her ladyship shook her head. "I don't know whether to laugh or to cry."

Edmund grinned broadly at her. " 'Tis always better to laugh," he advised.

Lady Mary chuckled. "Remember that in the weeks which lie ahead, for you may feel like crying yourself before we are done with you. If I had any doubts as to how much work lies ahead of us, your behavior this afternoon has put them to rest. We will begin educating you tonight."

Edmund's dinner that night was anything but enjoyable. If one woman did not find something distasteful in either his grammar or table manners, the other did. "Edmund, you must not make those horrible noises when you are eating your soup," said Lady Mary. "This is how you must take soup." She demonstrated.

Edmund imitated her and choked. " 'Tis a bloody pain trying to take my soup like that," he complained. "What's more, it ain't natural."

"It will be before we are done," said her ladyship. "And please do stop using that word."

Edmund made a face. "Treating me like a bloody child," he muttered.

"Edmund," reproved his aunt. "Your language. Please."

"Perhaps if you were to eat a little more slowly," added Susan helpfully, "it would be easier to be more quiet."

"Yes," said Lady Mary. "This is not a race to see who finishes first."

The next course arrived and Edmund dug in with hearty gusto. He looked across the table to see Susan looking at him in disgust. "What?" he demanded, his mouth full of food.

Edmund's newest gastronomic crime was obviously so horrible Susan couldn't bring herself to name it. "You must chew with your mouth shut," said Lady Mary.

Edmund flushed and Susan suddenly became very interested in something on the far side of the room. "I daresay we shall have nice weather again tomorrow," she said.

"I think, indeed, we shall," agreed her ladyship calmly. "And if it holds, perhaps you can show Edmund some of the sights." Edmund's face lit up. "After he has spent the morning learning about protocol," added his aunt. Edmund rolled his eyes and sighed, and Susan tried to look happy about the proposed outing.

The next day she dutifully showed him some of the sights that he most wanted to see. He enthusiastically dragged her about the city, taking her everywhere from the Tower of London to Weeks' Mechanical Museum. This last stop delighted Edmund to no end and he enthused about the mechanical birds and mice and other animals displayed. The mechanical tarantula convinced Susan they had seen enough and she shooed him out of the building and took him to Westminster Abbey. Edmund was properly awed by the overwhelming, Gothic structure, but upon leaving, insisted he much preferred the Mechanical Museum.

He had wanted to visit Tattersall's, but Susan refused, telling him he would have to visit that popular male haunt sometime when she was not with him. "Anyway," she said, climbing into Lady Mary's landau, "my feet hurt and I am tired. Surely Aunt Mary did not expect us to cover all of London in one day."

"I am sorry," said Edmund penitently. "I keep forgetting you city morts . . . er, ladies, ain't so strong as the country girls."

Susan took umbrage at this. "I was raised in the country," she said.

"Oh. Well, it must be because you are one of the . . ." He could feel his companion's critical eye on him and dodged the cant he had been about to use. "The upper class," he finished.

Susan said nothing, but it was plain that she didn't approve of this remark, either.

"Is there something about me you don't like?" asked Edmund.

Susan flushed deeply but made no reply, choosing instead to look out the carriage at the London bustle.

"What did I ever do to you?" he wondered.

"The first time we met you were kind enough to relieve me of my necklace," answered Susan.

"Well, other than that," he said.

Susan again looked away, refusing to comment.

"There is something more, isn't there?" demanded Edmund, but he still received no reply. "My aunt—" he began.

"*Your* aunt?" interrupted Susan coldly. "She is my aunt, but she certainly is not yours."

"She thinks she is," pointed out Edmund.

"Yes, she does, poor thing. She loved both Gerard and Edmund very much. She has wanted to believe all these years that Edmund was alive. And then you came along and took advantage—"

"What?"

"You are using her to feather your own nest," accused Susan.

"I? *I* am using *her*? It seems to me that I am the one who is being used. *Your* aunt don't like the present duke and she's using me to dethrone him, or whatever it is you do to dukes. I gave up a lot to do that."

"Oh, that is rich," said Susan. Their carriage had stopped in front of Lady Mary's town house, and even as the carriage steps were being let down they were still quarreling.

"You think I like this life?" demanded Edmund, following her up the walk. "It's 'Edmund, chew with your mouth shut,' and 'Edmund, stay in your room,' 'Edmund, you need new clothes'—"

"Which you were happy enough to get at my aunt's expense."

"She's getting her bloody pound's worth. I was happy as a gentleman's master," Edmund yelled as they entered the house.

"Oh! You would be," shot back Susan. "And call it what it really was. You were a robber, plain and simple!"

The faithful Harris pretended deafness during this exchange. "If Your Grace would care to join her ladyship in the drawing room? You have callers."

"Who the devil is it?" snarled Edmund.

"It is His Gr—" Harris halted, momentarily

stumped by a tricky situation. "It is her ladyship's cousin," he said.

Susan blanched. "Grayborough," she whispered.

4

"THE DUKE?" WHISPERED Edmund nervously.

Susan nodded.

Edmund looked at the drawing room door with distaste, but squared his shoulders and propelled himself and Susan toward it. "Best get it over with," he said.

Susan preceded Edmund into the room, and although she was not the one at whom it was directed, the angry look the Duke of Grayborough wore as he turned in his chair was enough to make her swallow nervously. The old man's reaction on seeing Edmund was even more upsetting. His anger turned to surprise and he began to gasp for breath, clutching at his chest. The man sitting next to him jumped from his chair and loosened the old man's cravat, calling for brandy.

Susan stood horrified, staring first at the gasping duke while Harris rushed by her, then at her aunt, who was looking at Edmund and smiling grimly. Susan turned to Edmund, but was too

late to see his reaction to the man he was depos-
ing, for he was already moving to help the duke.
"Here, let us lay him back against the cushions,"
said Edmund, reaching a helpful hand toward the
older man's shoulder.

The duke threw an arm out to fend the newcomer off and continued to gasp.

"He does not wish your help," said the other
man coldly.

Edmund backed away and into a chair.

Harris returned with the brandy. It was admin-
istered and the older man began to breathe more
steadily. Edmund sat regarding him and wondered, not for the first time, what he was doing
here. He certainly didn't belong with these nobs.
He obviously wasn't wanted. The duke was a
sour-looking fish if ever Edmund had seen one.
He had loose skin and a big belly and a thin,
irritable mouth. He was observing Edmund in a
very unwelcoming manner. The other man Edmund judged to be near his own age and must
be his second cousin Jarvis. He was a handsome
fellow with the same thin lips as his father, a
straight nose, and steely, gray eyes. He had a
strong jawline, which at the moment was set at
a pugnacious angle. Edmund smiled weakly.

"Where did you find this fellow?" demanded
the duke at last.

"I am sure you have already heard," said Lady
Mary.

"Then the rumors are true," said the duke. He
glowered at his new cousin. "I call it a cruel joke
to produce such an imposter and pawn him off

as Edmund," he said, turning his angry look on Lady Mary.

"You can look at him and call him an imposter?" demanded her ladyship.

"Of course he's an imposter," snapped the duke. "If Edmund was alive he would have been found years ago. I will grant you, this fellow has the look of Edmund."

"That is because he is Edmund," said Lady Mary calmly.

"Edmund is dead!" roared the duke. "You should have accepted that years ago, you dotty-headed female. Now you bring this . . . this . . . criminal into our midst, dress him in fine clothes and dub him Edmund and make our entire family the laughingstock of London. We shall have Cruikshank, Gilray, and every other idle fellow with a mischievous pen making light of us, and all because you happened upon a man who resembles Edmund. I'll not have it, Mary."

"Whether you will have it or not, Jonathan, I intend to see Edmund established as the rightful Duke of Grayborough," said Lady Mary. "If you will not step down of your own free will, then we shall leave it up to the lawyers to settle."

The duke's face turned apoplectic as he struggled to gain control of his temper. He failed and rose. "Until you come to your senses I have nothing further to say to you," he announced and stormed out of the room.

His son dutifully kissed Lady Mary's cheek and bid her farewell. He bowed over Susan's hand, said an equally polite good-bye, and followed his father.

Susan and Edmund both let out a sigh. "That was most unpleasant," said Susan.

"I knew it would be," said Lady Mary.

"Well, I didn't," said Edmund. "Both those fellows looked as if they'd like to cut out my gizzard."

"You can hardly blame my cousin for his ill manners," said her ladyship. "He has had the title these past fifteen years and has grown very attached to it, as well as to the fortune and rich lands that came with it. He will not easily give it up."

"I can," said Edmund. "I don't like this lay, not one bit. First thing tomorrow I'm leaving. You will have to find yourself another Edmund."

"I cannot," said Lady Mary. "There is no other save you and you know it."

"I do not!" cried Edmund.

"But you do. You must. I watched your face when you entered the room. I don't know what you are keeping from me, or from yourself, but this much I know, young man. You are Edmund. And you owe it to your family and to your brother's memory to step into his shoes."

Susan stared at Edmund. He looked panicked. "I tell you, I'm not your bloody Edmund!" he cried. He jumped up and began to pace. "I never saw that cull before, I tell you. And I ain't Edmund!" He took an angry swing at a nearby table and sent a Dresden shepherdess crashing to the floor. He stared at it a moment, as if trying to imagine how it had come to lie shattered at his feet. He looked at the ladies, who sat in shocked amazement, then pulled at his hair and with an anguished cry fled the room.

Lady Mary sighed and took a sip of tea, and Susan noticed now her hand shook as she lifted the cup to her lips. "Aunt Mary," she began gently.

"I know, child," said her aunt in a tired voice. "You think me mad. But I assure you, I am not. And I shall prove it. I have already proven it to Jonathan, which is why he is so upset. And I intend to prove it to all of London."

"But will Edmund remain to help you do so?" wondered Susan.

Lady Mary chewed her lip thoughtfully. "That remains to be seen." Again she sighed and leaned her head back against the sofa. "I suddenly feel very old. And tired. Perhaps I shall go lie down before dinner," she said, and got up with obvious effort.

"I am sure you will feel much better after a rest," said Susan consolingly.

Her aunt did, indeed, appear refreshed when she joined Susan for dinner that night. She had not looked happy when Harris delivered Edmund's message that he was unwell and would not be joining them, but she had recovered and now was doing justice to boiled potatoes, cauliflower, and a fine Portuguese ham. "I suppose he is up in his room drinking and pouting. I only hope he has not involved poor James in his shenanigans this time." Lady Mary shook her head. "We must get busy and find him a real valet. Where we will find a man brave enough, heaven knows."

"Are you sure he will stay?" ventured Susan.

"I am sure," said her ladyship. "I know he does not wish to, but I feel sure he will."

The two women spent a quiet evening together and retired early. But once in bed, Susan found herself thoroughly awake. Finally she crept downstairs in search of a book to lull herself to sleep.

She had gotten no farther than the foot of the stairs when the feeble light from her candle revealed a dark figure in the hall by the door. She let out a terrified gasp. The figure jumped, then rushed at her. Her gasp turned into a shriek, which the intruder cut short by clamping his hand over her mouth. Susan struggled with her captor, but only succeeded in losing her candle, which fell to the floor and left them in darkness. "Stubble it," he commanded. "It's me, Edmund." Then he angrily corrected himself. "Dick."

"Dick! Edmund!" she sputtered as soon as his hand left her mouth. "What do you think you are doing prowling around in the middle of the night, scaring people?"

"Sssh," he commanded. "Do you want to wake the whole house?"

Susan lowered her voice to an angry whisper. "What are you doing?" she demanded.

"I might ask you the same thing," retorted Edmund. "You scared the liver right out of me, sneaking up on me like that."

"I was not sneaking up on anyone. I came downstairs to find a book to read. Why are you here?"

"I'm leaving," said Edmund. "I left a note for Lady Mary. She will understand."

"I doubt she will," replied Susan scornfully. "For she is not a coward."

"I am not a coward," hissed Edmund, stung.

"Oh?"

The darkness hid the girl's face from him, but Edmund felt sure she was looking at him with contempt. "I don't belong here, I tell you," he insisted.

"Your aunt seems to think you do."

"My aunt!" Edmund peered nervously around him and lowered his voice. "That woman is not my aunt."

"You called her so earlier today," said Susan scornfully. "How do you know she is not your aunt? You said yourself you did not know who your parents were. She could be your aunt. And you could be Grayborough."

The girl had certainly sung a different tune earlier that day. "Why do you suddenly want me to be Grayborough?" demanded Edmund.

"Because my aunt wishes it," said Susan. "She believes you are Grayborough. Oh, can't you see what this means to her?" she said impatiently. "She never had children. Gerard and Edmund were everything to her. Finding Edmund has been what she's lived for these past few years. It is important to her to right what she feels is an old wrong, but it is even more important for her to find her nephew."

Edmund moaned and rubbed his head. "Was there ever a more unlucky fellow than I?" he soliloquized.

"There are many who would consider you very fortunate. It is not every man who is invited to step into a duke's shoes."

"This particular duke's shoes are already occupied," observed Edmund.

"Oh, go," cried Susan, pushing him back toward the door. "You are rude and stupid, and a great coward, and I am sure we will all be better off without you."

"And I *know* I will be better off without all of you!" retorted Edmund as he stumbled to the door.

Susan ran up the stairs and shut herself back in her room, where she paced for a good hour before crawling into a very cold bed. Here she lay, staring out her window and watching the moonbeams slowly turn to sunbeams.

She fell into a fitful sleep sometime after dawn. When she finally pulled herself from her bed it was with great effort. She dragged out her morning toilet as long as possible, but finally she could delay the moment no longer. She went down to breakfast prepared to console her aunt on the loss of her newfound nephew—and received a fresh shock.

Seated at the table and visiting with Lady Mary sat Edmund, looking appallingly fresh and rested. Susan stared at him in disbelief and he grinned at her.

"Susan, love, you look as if you didn't sleep a wink," said her ladyship.

"I did sleep poorly," admitted Susan, turning to the sideboard. "Something woke me and I could not get back to sleep afterward."

"I am sorry. Perhaps you can rest this afternoon," suggested Lady Mary kindly. "I was just giving Edmund a lesson in etiquette. I had thought you might be willing to help him with the steps to the waltz this morning, but if you are not feeling up to it we can begin his dancing lessons tomorrow."

"I should be happy to help him this morning," said Susan, and the look on her face told Edmund the only happiness she would receive from this task would come from having an opportunity to step on his foot.

"Excellent," declared Lady Mary enthusiastically. "I have some important correspondence to see to and then I shall join you."

The room dubbed the ballroom in Lady Mary's townhouse was smaller than most, but when only occupied by two people it looked exceptionally big. Edmund and Susan's voices echoed unnaturally as they entered the deserted room. "I thought you were leaving us, Your Grace," she said.

"I decided to stay on," replied Edmund. " 'Tis a good lay and I'd be a fool to leave it."

"And that is the only reason you remain, because it is a 'good lay'?" demanded Susan scornfully.

The new duke obviously had a tough hide that couldn't be pierced by a woman's scorn. He smiled at her and his smile seemed to taunt her. "There are many reasons why I remain, fair Susan." He took a step nearer to her and brushed her bare arm with his fingers.

She blushed and moved away. "I am sure my

aunt will be happy to know you plan to stay with us," she said.

Susan's voice and manner were all business as they began his dancing lesson, but she soon became engrossed in his progress, and with each new step he mastered, a little more ice melted from her voice. Soon she was talking to him in friendly and encouraging tones.

Edmund could hardly be blamed for mistaking the enthusiasm and encouragement of a natural teacher for something else. As they waltzed across the floor and he became more comfortable with the steps, his mind was free to focus on his partner and he began pulling her into an ever-closer embrace. Smiling down at her, he began to hum. She returned the smile, then looked coquettishly away. The little vixen—pretending to be shy! That skin was exquisite, so invitingly smooth. That graceful, long neck, those lips . . . The wide circle in which they had been moving shrank and Edmund brought them slowly to a stop. "You really are a beautiful woman," he murmured, and as she blushed he kissed her.

Susan's blush deepened into an angry flush and she pulled back from him. "You must never do that again," she scolded.

"But you wanted me to," protested Edmund.

Susan gasped. "I most certainly did not!" she cried.

Edmund fixed a piercing stare on his dance partner, which made her blush even more deeply. "At the Blue Boar men and women were more honest about their feelings," he said.

Susan raised her chin to a haughty angle. "May I remind you, sir, that you are no longer an intimate of the Blue Boar? I suggest you adjust your behavior accordingly. The first lady on whom you try that little trick will have you at the altar before the cat can lick her ear."

Edmund slipped his arms around her waist. "And does that apply to you as well, fair Susan?"

Susan took a step back and took his right hand firmly in hers. "I think we had best try the steps again," she said.

Lady Mary's arrival on the scene prevented Edmund from misbehaving further and the rest of the lesson proceeded without incident.

"Your pupil is making excellent progress," said Lady Mary the following day as the two women strolled along Oxford Street. "Will he be ready to make his appearance at Almack's this Wednesday?"

"Oh, yes," replied Susan unenthusiastically.

"You are still not enamored of our protégé," guessed her ladyship.

"Our protégé is a conceited rakehell," said Susan irritably. Immediately contrite, she begged her aunt's pardon.

Lady Mary smiled. "He should fit into our noble ranks quite well, then."

Susan said nothing but kept her jaw clamped tightly shut.

"Why do you not care for my nephew?" asked her ladyship.

Susan opened her mouth to speak then shut it on a sigh.

"You may be frank, child."

"Dear aunt, I cannot believe this man to be your nephew. He is rough and uncultured and—"

"And he has made ungentlemanly advances?" guessed her ladyship. The ever-ready blush rose to Susan's cheeks and her ladyship chuckled. "Edmund is a bit rough around the edges, but he is a good man." Her niece made a face at this, but Lady Mary ignored it. "The boy I knew is still alive in the man, buried under years of hardship and lack of proper guidance, but there all the same. Time will prove that, I am sure."

Susan remained unconvinced, and as if to prove her right, Edmund behaved abominably at his social debut at Almack's. He demonstrated his skill as a pickpocket to a group of young bucks and horrified the most toplofty of Almack's patronesses, Mrs. Drummond Burrell, who happened to be standing nearby. She, in turn, horrified Lady Mary by vowing to bar Edmund from the rooms if he did not mend his ways instantly.

Lady Mary took him in hand and gave him a stern lecture. She finally let him leave her side only to have him plunge immediately into trouble again. He became carried away when dancing with an extremely flirtatious lady, giving her an appreciative pinch and receiving only a squeal and a slap in return. Her husband was no more understanding than his wife had been and challenged Edmund to a duel. Only some very fast talking, which Lady Mary expertly dissolved into tears and pleading, caused the irate lord to change his mind. Here again, Edmund was no help, for the prospect of a good fight appealed to him as much as it did to his challenger. Lady Mary was finally forced to the use of diversionary tactics and announced the beginnings of severe heart palpitations.

Jarvis and Susan watched the brangle from across the room, one with concern, the other with scorn. "One wonders why our eccentric relation chose to conjure up the missing Edmund," said Jarvis. "Boredom, perhaps? The fellow certainly is entertaining, if nothing else." Susan made no comment. "My dear Miss Montague, do not tell me you find this fellow amusing!" said Jarvis in disbelief.

"Of course not!" exclaimed Susan. "But Aunt is convinced he is Edmund, and if that is the case I feel we should at least allow him a little time to find his feet." Jarvis said nothing, but his smile mocked her. "If you will excuse me, I am sure my aunt must need me," she said frostily and left him.

Jarvis watched her go and the smile on his face was not a pleasant one.

"You simply cannot behave in the ballroom as you would in the taproom," scolded Lady Mary as she and Susan took their embarrassing charge home. "You are the Duke of Grayborough and your title demands—"

"Damn the title!" interrupted Edmund. "I never asked to be a bloody duke. I was perfectly happy as Dick White."

"I am sure you were," agreed his aunt calmly. "But Dick White is not who you really are.

You are Edmund Morris Worthington, Duke of Grayborough. And when the proper time comes I shall prove it to the world at large and to you as well."

5

WHILE EDMUND WAITED to prove his claim to the title the ton amused themselves by taking up sides. Was the newcomer the real Duke of Grayborough? Many felt his star was on the rise and his friendship worth cultivating. Others sided with the present duke and chose to ignore the rough diamond who had come among them.

When questioned, the present duke was usually heard to proclaim that his cousin Lady Mary had not been herself lately and that this most recent freakish behavior was a prime example of an unhinged brain.

His son, the young man who had spent most of his life as the son of a duke, did not appear any more overjoyed to have his long-lost cousin restored to the family bosom than was his father. Many of his acquaintance had taken a liking to the good-natured Edmund, catching him up in the social whirl, taking him to Boodles and Watier's, attending cock fights with him and including him in their Bond Street lounging. Of course, Jarvis's closest friends remained loyal and shunned the newcomer, but they were not above teasing Jarvis.

He appeared to have little sense of humor when it came to his cousin. At Lady Waverly's rout he stood watching Edmund as he talked with two men on the other side of the room. Edmund had obviously made some jest, as his companions began to laugh uproariously. Jarvis scowled.

"He's not such a bad sort," admitted Jarvis's crony, Lord Piking, following his friend's gaze. "Rotten luck, though," he added consolingly.

"You sound as if the case has already been decided in his favor," accused Jarvis.

"Oh, no, no," said his friend. "Everyone knows the issue cannot be decided till you all meet with the lawyers."

"Then perhaps you might save your consolations until such time as I need them?" snapped Jarvis.

Piking nodded and wisely changed the subject.

Edmund knew he was the center of controversy. He also knew many of his new friends would drop him like a hot coal if his claim was not proved. If that happened Edmund wouldn't mourn the loss of his new life much. He'd return to haunt the Blue Boar and be welcomed with open arms by those who truly loved him. He had to admit he would miss the old lady, though. He had grown quite fond of her. But the opinion of the ton mattered little to him.

Save Lady Mary, there was only one other person in London for whose opinion he cared. "Do you think I am really Edmund?" he asked Susan as they rode along a Hyde Park bridle path one morning.

"Aunt Mary says you are," she answered evasively.

"But what do you think?" he persisted.

"What I think cannot matter," she said.

"It matters to me," said Edmund.

Susan looked straight ahead, avoiding his searching eyes. "I tell you honestly," she said at last. "I do not know what to think. I find it hard to believe that an orphan who has spent his adult life," she paused, searching for words, "as you have," she continued diplomatically, "could be the same person my aunt lost so many years ago. Yet she seems to have found some irrefutable proof which makes her sure of you."

"I know the likes of you could have nothing to do with me if I were a commoner," said Edmund. "But if it turns out I am indeed Grayborough—"

He was prevented from finishing his sentence by the approach of his cousin, Jarvis. "Now what does he want?" grumbled Edmund.

Jarvis fell in beside them. "Miss Montague, good day," he said pleasantly. "Edmund." The nod was polite but the voice cold, and Edmund made no reply.

"How are you this morning?" asked Susan politely.

"I am fine now I have seen you," said Jarvis. "Riding about Hyde Park alone is a tedious business."

"Then why don't you go home?" suggested Edmund.

Susan gave him a reprimanding look and turned back to Jarvis. "You weren't quite alone, I believe. Wasn't that Lord Alvanley I saw you with just a moment ago?"

Jarvis shrugged aside his noble companion. "Alvanley can hardly count as company. He hasn't your eyes," he finished with a teasing smile.

Susan blushed and lowered her eyes.

Edmund frowned. "Her eyes, as well as the rest of her, are busy with me at the moment."

"Precisely why I am here. The poor girl looked very much in need of rescuing. Most ladies like to be rescued from highwaymen, do they not?"

Edmund's complexion turned a deep red as he glared at his new cousin. "Let us at least put the emphasis where it belongs, on the word 'man.' Better a highwayman than a man-milliner."

Now it was Jarvis's turn to flush angrily.

"Please," begged Susan. She reached out and laid an imploring hand on Jarvis's arm. "Is this any way for cousins to behave?"

"It has not yet been proven we are cousins," replied Jarvis. He turned a superior look on Edmund. "If you are lucky, after this is all settled we may allow you to wear the Grayborough livery, but that is the closest you will ever come to the title—gutter boy." With that he bid Susan good day and cantered away.

"Yes, well I might do the same for you," Edmund called after him. "Conceited fellow. What makes him think he's made of better cloth than the rest of us, anyway?"

Susan sighed. "It is the way the nobility are. You must not mind him. He is, naturally, upset by your sudden appearance. If you are made duke it will affect his future."

"He is a lord. Surely that cannot be taken from him," said Edmund, feeling no sympathy.

"That is not quite right," corrected Susan patiently. "If you become Grayborough his father will be reduced back to an earl and your cousin will then be a merely a viscount."

"Sob, sob. 'Tis breaking my heart to hear this," mocked Edmund.

"I am not asking you to feel sorry for your cousin," said Susan. "I am simply asking you to understand. It is no small thing to lose a dukedom. And the Grayborough fortune is as impressive as the title. It is a hard prize to give up."

Edmund shook his head. "Everyone I have met lives a life I only dreamed of having, yet none of them seem content. Their hands are full but they all grab for more."

"I am afraid you are right," agreed Susan. "But it is the way of things so you must not be too hard on him. And you must remember, this is all very unexpected. Everyone thought Edmund dead. Your cousin grew up with the understanding he would be the next duke. Now, suddenly, here you are, a stranger, claiming what he has always assumed to be his. And the fact that you were, er . . . Your particular past makes your claim to the title all the more galling. I can hardly blame him for finding this rather hard to accept."

"It is not only my cousin who finds my past galling, is it?" asked Edmund softly.

Susan's face turned a soft pink and she lowered her eyes. "I suppose you cannot be blamed for having fallen in with bad company," she said doubtfully.

"I did what I did to survive," said Edmund. He sighed. "I suppose I am not so proud of my life now. At the time it all seemed a lark. And stealing from the nobs did not seem so horrible."

"I should think stealing from anyone horrible."

Edmund hung his head. "I should think you are right," he agreed.

And after considerable thought he decided she was also right about his attitude toward his cousin. He shouldn't be so hard on the fellow. So when Edmund and his friend Mr. Fortescue visited Jackson's boxing saloon and encountered his cousin, Edmund was perfectly willing to be conciliatory. Never mind that the fellow was a cold fish, that he obviously hated Edmund, that he obviously liked Susan. They could possibly be related. Edmund would be nice to him. And wouldn't the fair Susan be proud of him? "Hallo there, cousin," he called pleasantly as he and Fortescue sauntered into the room.

Jarvis was stripped to the waist, waiting to have a go with the Gentleman, himself. His look was not welcoming.

Edmund tried again. "Going to have a go of it, eh?"

"Yes, I am, *cousin.*" The word sounded insultingly like a sneer. Jarvis looked Edmund up and down. "Are you a pugilist now as well as a gentleman?"

Male feathers began to ruffle. "I was always good with my daddles," said Edmund.

"I'll wager you were," said Fortescue heartily. "Well, come on old fellow. Let's go shake off some of these togs, shall we?"

Edmund ignored his friend and remained where he was, his look challenging his cousin.

"Perhaps you would care to demonstrate your skills now?" suggested Jarvis.

"Perhaps I would," agreed Edmund, struggling out of his coat and throwing it on the floor. Shirt and cravat followed, tossed after the coat with equal carelessness.

"I say," objected Fortescue. "Have a care for the cloth, man. You won't want to be seen in rumpled rags."

His words went unheeded. Edmund was already out on the floor with his cousin, fists raised.

It was not a friendly match. Jarvis's punches were fast and hard and well aimed, and his superior training showed. Before ten minutes had passed Edmund was sporting a swollen, purpling eye and a cut lip and a very sore abdomen.

With a new hit to the lip and the drawing of fresh blood, survival became all important. As quickly as he had cast off his gentleman's clothes Edmund now cast off a gentleman's rules for fighting and resorted to methods he knew would end his suffering. He brought a knee to his cousin's groin. Jarvis doubled in pain and Edmund delivered an uppercut to the chin that threw Jarvis back and knocked him cold.

Edmund stood panting over his adversary, adrenaline pumping a wild feeling of triumph through him. He expected applause, cheers, shouts of congratulations . . . at least from Fortescue. There was silence. Edmund looked around. It was a shocked silence.

Edmund wiped the blood from his lip with the back of his hand and backed away from his fallen cousin. As the blue haze of rage retreated he could see he had made a grave social error.

"I say," said Fortescue in an undertone. "A low blow like that just ain't done."

"Well, it is where I come from," said Edmund. "If I must choose between being polite and keeping my blood inside my body I had rather not be polite."

"Best spill a little blood," advised his friend. "A man without honor soon finds himself without friends."

Edmund sighed. "I'd as lief return to being a highwayman," he muttered.

But Fortescue was right. Jarvis was supposed to be his cousin, after all. If Susan got wind of this she'd give him a regular bear garden jaw. And he'd deserve it. Suddenly penitent, he knelt beside the moaning Jarvis and slapped him gently on the cheek. "Wake up, coz. Nap time is finished."

Jarvis opened his eyes. He blinked and took a try at propping himself up on one elbow.

Edmund tried to apologize while his cousin gingerly tested his jaw. "Sorry, old fellow. For a moment there I quite thought you wanted to fight to the death."

The look Jarvis gave Edmund said he would have liked to have done just that.

"I suppose I let myself get carried away," said Edmund, still trying to mend fences. He put out a hand to help his cousin up but Jarvis ignored it and struggled to his feet unaided.

He looked at Edmund haughtily. "I suppose you did, *Your Grace*." The words were said scornfully and Edmund stiffened. "Further proof," continued Jarvis, "that your claim to the title is not only bogus but ridiculous."

With that he left Edmund angrily clenching his hands into fists.

6

EDMUND INSPECTED HIMSELF in his looking glass before going down to the drawing room for tea. His lip was twice its normal size and one eye was a bilious purple-green and swollen up like a frog's. "Well, I've looked worse," he said.

James, the footman turned valet, looked dubious.

"I have," boasted Edmund. "These London man-milliners think they know how to fight, but I know any one of ten men who could tear one apart in five minutes. Can you guess how that impertinent cousin managed to give me this?" He pointed to his eye and the mesmerized James shook his head. "I was trying to fight like a gentleman, that's how. The minute I got serious about the matter he was down." James looked properly impressed and Edmund held up his hands. "A man who is good with his fives can make his way just fine in the world."

James nodded his agreement. "And I suppose a man could scare away a rival if he was good with his hands," he ventured.

"Easily," agreed Edmund. He looked thoughtfully at James. "Are you good with your hands, old fellow?"

James flushed and mumbled a disclaimer.

"Come on. Let us see. Show me your best fighting stance."

James shuffled his feet and looked bashful and said he couldn't bother his grace.

"No, no. Come on, now." Edmund pointed to his chin. "See if you can plant one right here. Put up your daddles."

The two men squared off. "That is not bad," said Edmund encouragingly as they circled each other. "Now, plant me a facer."

James swung and Edmund dodged. "Footwork, footwork!" called Edmund. "Look what you are doing with your feet."

Edmund looked at what James was doing with his feet and James threw a punch. Edmund fell back with a yelp and James let out a gasp. "Your Grace, your eye! Are you hurt?" He watched Edmund staggering, holding a hand to his previously unharmed eye, and bit his lip, waiting for his dismissal without references.

Edmund bent and shook his head. "If that ain't a good one on me," he laughed. "You have quite a punch there, slap me if you don't. A regular Tom Cribb." He clapped his amazed valet on the back. "Do you know, I think we could make quite a fighter out of you." He looked at James speculatively. "James, old fellow, have you ever thought of taking this up seriously?"

"Whatever can be keeping Edmund?" wondered his aunt. "It is not like him to be late for dinner."

"Perhaps he is not yet returned," suggested Susan.

Lady Mary rang for Harris. "Has my nephew returned?" she asked.

"I believe so, Your Ladyship," said Harris, not revealing by so much as a raised eyebrow that His Grace had indeed returned and upset the entire staff by convincing a starry-eyed James that he had a future as a pugilist.

"Very good, Harris," she said and dismissed the butler. "We shan't wait for him," she told her niece.

At that moment the subject of their conversation entered the room. Susan, who sat facing the door, gasped. Lady Mary turned, and on sight of Edmund gasped also. "Edmund! What have you done to yourself?" she demanded.

"Oh, nothing," he replied airily, hoping to skirt the details of his earlier encounter with his cousin and protect his valet as well. "Just a little to-do at Jackson's."

"Little?" His aunt looked on him in disgust. "And where are we to take you looking like this?"

Edmund hung his head.

Lady Mary gave an exasperated sigh. "Do stop standing about like a naughty nursery brat and let us have our dinner," she said. "This is just one more thing to set the ton on its ear, but I am used to being a laughingstock by now."

Edmund was truly penitent. "I am sorry. I am afraid I did not think."

"As usual," muttered Susan, and he glared at her.

He took his aunt's hand. "I can stay in for a few days," he offered.

"No." Lady Mary shook her head. "I suppose you will not be the first young buck to attend a rout with a blackened eye." A reluctant grin appeared on her ladyship's face. "Or two," she added. "By the bye," she said, "Harris tells me he knows of an excellent valet looking for a position."

"I should prefer to keep James," said Edmund.

"But would he prefer to remain with you is the question," said her ladyship. "Your blackened eyes remind me of a certain attack upon the young man that he may not wish to have repeated."

Edmund's eye was still smarting. "I am sure it won't be," he said with a smile.

That night at Lady Henry's rout Miss Ravenscort asked with horror what had happened to his grace.

Edmund caught a glimpse of Lady Mary across the room. If he told Miss Ravenscort he had been fighting at Jackson's she might press him for more details, and if his aunt heard he had been fighting with his cousin she would give him a regular tongue lashing. What to do? "Footpads," said Edmund, improvising.

"Footpads," echoed Miss Ravenscort with awe.

"Three of 'em," added Edmund, warming to his subject. "Big, ugly fellows. One had a scar. Right here." He pointed to his forehead.

"How did you ever fight them off? Were you alone?"

Edmund nodded. "It was a fierce battle, I can tell you. I tripped one and he landed at my feet. Another—"

"Hello, Miss Ravenscort," said a soft voice at his elbow.

"Susan!" Edmund felt his face grow uncomfortably hot.

She raised a delicate eyebrow. "What interesting escapade are you recounting to Miss Ravenscort?" she asked.

"Oh, nothing, nothing," said Edmund. "Are you thirsty?"

"Not particularly," said Susan. She smiled at Miss Ravenscort, encouraging her to tell all.

"His Grace was telling me about his attack by the footpads. It was most terrible."

"Footpads?" echoed a passing young lady. "Was someone attacked by footpads?"

"His Grace was set upon by footpads only last night," said Miss Ravenscort. "It is a wonder he is even alive."

"Is that how you got your eyes blackened?" asked the other young lady.

There was no turning back now. Edmund nodded, feeling Susan's eyes upon him. "Are you sure you are not thirsty?" he asked her.

"Perhaps a little. Aunt is looking for you," she added.

Edmund shot her a grateful smile and excused himself from his feminine admirers. "Did my aunt really wish to see me?" he asked as he made good his escape.

"No," replied Susan shortly.

"Thank you," he murmured.

"I don't know why I help you," she said in exasperation. "For I have never seen a man less deserving of help."

"Here now!" protested Edmund.

"Now you will look a pretty fool when it is discovered you have been making that up," she predicted. "Footpads, indeed!"

"Well, I couldn't tell her the truth. If word got back to my aunt I'd been fighting with my noble cousin I should be in trouble, indeed."

"So that is how your eyes got blackened," said Susan crossly. "If word gets out you are a braggart and a liar you will be in even worse trouble," she scolded.

"You are right," admitted Edmund. "I shall never fit in this society."

Susan said nothing to reassure him. "Why ever did you fight with him?" she asked in exasperation.

"It was not I who started it," protested Edmund. "I must say I am heartily sick of this habit of yours of always assuming the worst about me. I tried to be friendly with the fellow, but he'd have none of it. Hates me. God knows why."

"I have already explained to you why he hates you," said Susan wearily.

"It is not as if the fellow will be living on the streets. He has property."

"Oh, really. There is no talking to you," said Susan.

"Not if you insist on always judging me before hearing my side of a story," agreed Edmund.

Susan looked at Edmund, stunned. "Is that what you think I do?"

"Isn't it?" he countered.

She fell silent a moment. "Perhaps, sometimes it is," she said softly.

"If you had grown up on the streets of London how would you behave and think? Would it be the same as you do now?"

"You did not grow up on the streets of London," said Susan irritably.

"No, I did not. But I definitely did not grow up in the same world as you, so how can you expect me to act in the same way?"

As Susan had no ready answer for this question Edmund left her in search of punch. She watched him go, a thoughtful look on her face.

At the punch bowl Edmund met yet another who misjudged him. Jarvis was sporting a faintly green jaw. He greeted his cousin with a cynical grin. "The footpads you boast of fighting must have given you the other black eye."

Edmund refused to be baited. He raised his chin and replied haughtily, "No. My valet gave me the other."

"I can see why you wish everyone to think you were set upon by footpads."

"I doubt you can see anything at all," said Edmund. "You are a selfish, spoilt fool, and if you think I care what you or any of your priggish friends think you are very much mistaken."

"Why else would you make up such a story?" scoffed Jarvis.

"To keep my aunt from finding out I brangled with my cousin, you dolt," snapped Edmund. He looked scornfully at the other man. "I have grown up hard and learned things you and your friends only pretend to know. I could have beat you to a bloody pulp. I didn't. God alone knows why I tell you this. I am tired of trying to befriend you. If you wish to be enemies then so be it. I'll take that bloody title you've been planning to inherit and the fortune that goes with it and laugh in your face." Edmund scooped up his cup of punch. He marched back to Susan and thrust it at her, spilling punch in the process. Eyes wide, she took it. "Here. Drink your punch," he commanded. "Then please be so good as to tell my aunt I wish to leave at her earliest convenience."

Such a high-in-the-instep, dukelike speech. Who would have thought to hear such refined haughtiness from the mouth of Dickie Boy White? A small smile lifted one corner of Edmund's mouth. That had felt rather good. And it had come so easily. Perhaps, just perhaps . . . Don't be ridiculous, he scolded himself. Let them think whatever they wish, but you, old boy, had best keep the truth in front of you, else you will surely go mad.

With this thought firmly in mind, he rode with his aunt two weeks later to the Worthington family town house, rightful property of the Duke of Grayborough. Whatever the outcome of the meeting with the lawyers this day, he should come about. But what of her? He studied the woman sitting across from him. She was looking out the window, but he felt sure it was not the streets of Mayfair she was seeing. Scenes from the past, both melancholy and merry, danced before her.

As if sensing his eyes on her, she turned and smiled at him. "Are you nervous?" she asked.

Edmund shook his head. "No. Are you?"

"No. But I must admit I am excited. I have waited long for this day."

"I hope, for your sake, you will not be disappointed," said Edmund.

She smiled at him and shook her head. "You really do not know, do you?"

Edmund's brows knit.

"Never mind," she said. "For some reason the past is lost to you." She leaned forward and took his hand. "But it will soon be found. And I pray you will not hate me for resurrecting it."

"And I pray you will not hate me if what you wish to claim for me turns out not to be mine," he said, squeezing her hand.

The carriage stopped, and Edmund and his aunt alighted and walked into the London residence of the present Duke of Grayborough, where the past waited to be searched and the future to be changed.

7

EDMUND AND HIS aunt were ushered into the library. A table occupied the center of the room. At it sat a collection of lawyers—Lady Mary's own man, Mr. Townsend, and his junior partner; and next to them an old man with a ramrod back, intently studying the papers that lay before him. At the arrival of the claimant all rose and polite greetings were exchanged. "Old Apperton himself," Lady Mary whispered to Edmund. "He has handled the affairs of the family for years." And she smiled as if this were something in their favor.

Standing in a corner of the room, looking uncomfortable and self-conscious, stood an old man and a woman, obviously former servants of some sort. At the sight of Edmund their eyes widened and they looked at each other.

Jarvis had been lounging against the mantelpiece and came forward to greet her ladyship with a kiss.

"Good day, Jarvis," she said briskly. "You are looking well for a young man whose future hangs in the balance." Jarvis shrugged carelessly and she continued. "I hope you realize there has been no malice intended you by my pursuit of Edmund these years past. I seek only to right an old wrong."

Jarvis nodded his understanding.

"Where is your father?" she asked.

"He should be here momentarily."

As if on cue, the present duke made his entrance. Unlike some men his age, he had not clung to the fashions of his youth. The Duke of Worthington had enjoyed his considerable fortune, and keeping up with fashion had been one of many pleasures with which he had indulged himself. His frock coat was of bath superfine and his buff pantaloons were a perfect fit. His cravat was blindingly white and simply arranged and was held in place with a large, pearl pin. He entered the room like a king granting an audience rather than a man whose right to a title was being seriously challenged. "Mary, I am glad to see you on time. Perhaps we can be done with this business as soon as possible," he said.

"That will suit me fine," agreed Lady Mary. "I see we are still missing one person."

His grace looked around. "All the principals seem to be present. We certainly do not lack for lawyers."

Her ladyship turned to Mr. Townsend. "Where is Miss Bird?"

"I have sent a man to fetch her. She should arrive at any moment," replied Mr. Townsend.

"Bird? Bird?" repeated his grace. "Who is this Miss Bird?"

"You would not remember her, Jonathan," said her ladyship. "She was nurse to the Worthington children."

"So that's your game, is it?" burst out the duke. "No papers, no proper legal proof, so you have resorted to bribing an old nurse into recognizing this fellow as the long-lost Edmund. Faugh! It sickens me."

"That is not what sickens you," retorted Lady Mary. "It is the fact that you yourself know him to be Edmund, and now I have provided others who can identify him as well and take from you what was never yours."

Mr. Apperton cleared his throat. "Perhaps Your Grace would care to be seated," he suggested. "This could prove a long and tiring morning."

His Grace stamped to the table and deposited himself in a chair, looking more like a pouting child than a duke.

Unruffled by her relation's bad manners, Lady Mary moved to greet the two old retainers still hovering uncertainly at the corner of the room. "I wish to thank you for coming," she said.

"There is no need to thank us. We only want to see the boy get what he deserves," said the man.

Now another player made her entrance onto the stage. "It is Miss Bird," announced Lady Mary unnecessarily. The woman was well-suited to her name. In spite of the fact that she was bent with arthritis, she seemed to hop into the room. White curls peeped out from under the little lady's bonnet and her tiny face was softly lined, but her black eyes sparkled, betraying a mind still safe from the ravages of age. She cocked her head much like a robin and inspected the room. She regarded Edmund with those little bright eyes and a smile curved the thin lips. The bright eyes grew brighter still. "Master Edmund!" she exclaimed.

Edmund politely stepped up to her and shook her hand.

"Master Edmund, do you not remember me? Tis I, Birdie!" she prompted.

Edmund's brow furrowed in concentration. He made a mental grab for something dancing just at the edge of his mind's eye and missed. He shook his head. "I am sorry," he said. "I am afraid I do not remember you."

"You haven't coached your pupil very well," scoffed His Grace from the table.

Mr. Apperton cleared his throat. "If everyone is here, perhaps we may begin?"

"By all means," agreed Her Ladyship, seating herself at the table.

Edmund sat next to her, and as he waited for his fate to be decided he couldn't help thinking how much simpler life would have been if he'd remained a highwayman. All these people who claimed to know him, wanting him to remember them. And he didn't, couldn't. Why had he ever stopped that bloody coach?

"We realize the claimant has no papers of any kind with which to prove he is Edmund Morris Worthington, rightful Duke of Grayborough," Mr. Apperton was saying.

"It must also be taken into consideration that, although the claimant was finally pronounced dead, no body was ever produced to prove that death beyond all shadow of a doubt. If the claimant had, under great emotion, fled his home, he would not have had the forethought to take with him any proof of his identity," put in Mr. Townsend. "Which is why Her Ladyship has produced these witnesses." He turned to the old couple, who were still standing and looking ill at ease. "Mr. and Mrs. Harding. You were the gatekeepers at Grayborough Hall, were you not?"

The old man nodded.

"And does this young man look familiar to you?"

Again the old man nodded.

"Can you please tell us why?"

"He has the mark," said the man.

"Please explain yourself," prompted the lawyer.

"The birthmark. On his cheek. Master Edmund had just such a mark."

"Many people have birthmarks," observed the duke. "This is no proof."

"He has the coloring of the young master, too," added the man when further prompted.

"And Mrs. Harding, would you concur with your husband's testimony?" asked the lawyer. She looked at him in confusion. The lawyer framed his question more simply. "Do you agree with him?"

"He does have the same mark as Mr. Edmund. I fancy this is what the master would look like as a grown man," she said. "In fact, I am sure . . . Oh, Master Edmund, do you not remember me? You used to come to visit and eat gingerbread boys."

Edmund looked helplessly at the woman. He wished for her sake he did remember. But more than anything he wished he were not sitting at this table with all these people staring at him.

"How very odd that Edmund Worthington has no memory of his life as a child," murmured Jarvis.

Edmund shot him an angry glance, but he was feeling the same thing, himself. Why couldn't he remember?

"If you had experienced something as horrible as Edmund had, perhaps you would choose to forget it also," reprimanded Lady Mary.

Edmund's head began to ache. Accidental shooting. Death. Oh, dear God, his brother! He felt sick.

The lawyer was now questioning Miss Bird. Again the birthmark on Edmund's face was discussed, as well as his features and coloring. "Is there anything else, any distinct physical feature you might know of that could be useful in identifying this man as the lost heir to the Grayborough title?" asked Mr. Townsend.

The little lady nodded eagerly. "Yes, there is one. Of course, not many people would know about it. I do because I was the one who changed his . . ." She stopped, blushing. "It is in a most unusual spot."

Edmund could feel his face turning crimson. He knew exactly to what Miss Bird was referring. He had certainly taken his share of teasing about it over the years. The women he bedded had found it as amusing as they had charming. One wench had taken to calling him Sweetheart and had spread the news of how very much like a heart the small red mark on his buttocks looked. He began to squirm. They were all looking at him expectantly. "I won't show it to no one," he burst out, his agitation forcing him to lapse into bad grammar.

"Of course he won't," scoffed the duke. "He has no such mark."

"If he were to have such a uniquely placed mark," continued Mr. Townsend, ignoring this interchange, "I believe we could all agree this would be conclusive proof of the gentleman's true identity." He looked questioningly at the other lawyer, who nodded his agreement, then turned to Edmund. "Perhaps you would be so good as to repair to another room with us?"

Not even for a dukedom would Edmund show that embarrassing mark. He sat rooted to his seat.

"Edmund, you must," said his aunt. "This is too important a matter for you to turn missish."

Edmund looked around the room at the faces regarding him. The old retainers looked at him lovingly, the duke was openly scoffing, and his son looked equally cynical. "I remember that mark," he said. "His brother used to tease him about it. No wonder this fellow is reluctant to cooperate. It is the one thing an imposter could not imitate."

Edmund glared at him and rose from the table. Mr. Townsend turned to the duke. "Perhaps Your Grace would allow us the use of . . . ?"

"Take them to one of the guest rooms," growled the duke to his son. "And remain as a witness."

"Oh, no. I'll not have him in there," said Edmund, pointing angrily at his cousin.

"Edmund!" His aunt's voice was sharp. He turned a mutinous face to her. "Please," she said.

Edmund made no reply. He stalked from the room, followed by the lawyers and Jarvis.

An uncomfortable silence fell. The duke favored Lady Mary with a glare, then chose to ignore her presence. His malevolence did not ruffle her ladyship's calm. She sat and smiled, comfortably smug.

The first one to return to the room was Jarvis. His face was pale and his eyes looked wild. He turned those wild eyes to his father, who looked at him in horror, then grabbed the table. The lawyers had now entered the room and were speaking softly to each other, shuffling papers and fussing with quills. Mr. Apperton turned and attempted to speak to the duke, but the duke was in no condition to hear him. His face was purpling dangerously. "This is an outrage!" he roared.

"This is the truth," said Lady Mary triumphantly. "And well you know it, Jonathan."

The former duke rose and shook his cane angrily at Lady Mary. He opened his mouth to speak but no sound came out. His eyebrows peaked in pain and his open mouth twisted. He grabbed at his chest and collapsed across the table.

8

"FETCH A DOCTOR!" barked Jarvis and someone rushed from the room in search of a footman. Son tenderly laid father back in his chair and loosened his cravat.

Edmund stood staring in horror at the fallen man. The former duke's skin looked an alarming shade of gray. Edmund edged toward the pair, uncertain as to what he could do to help but wishing to do something.

Jarvis glared at him, and his aunt tugged at his arm. "Come. There is nothing we can do here." She turned to their lawyer as she propelled Edmund out the door. "I am sure there will be papers and other matters to attend to. Perhaps you will call on His Grace later in the week?"

"Of course," murmured the lawyer.

The new Duke of Grayborough allowed himself to be led away from the alarming scene in the library and out of the townhouse. "This is my fault," he said once they were inside their carriage.

"It is no more your fault than it is mine," said her ladyship. "My cousin owes his present state to no one but himself. It is his stubbornness and greed that has brought on this attack, and if I know Jonathan he will survive it just to spite us all. He would certainly not want to give you the satisfaction of dying and allowing you an unalloyed enjoyment of the dukedom."

Edmund rubbed his aching head. Both position and great wealth, funded and landed, were suddenly his. He was now responsible for a large estate peopled by who knew how many dependents, and he knew nothing of crops and cattle. He had a town house, a hunting lodge, and heaven knew how many servants. He was the head of a large and important family, none of whom he remembered. And he had killed his brother. Edmund silently cursed the mark that had brought him to this pass. I bear the mark, but I am not Edmund, he thought. Not anymore. "I should never have entered your carriage," he sighed miserably.

"Surely you can no longer doubt your true identity," said his aunt.

"My true identity is who I have been these years past," said Edmund. "I cannot be nobility. I was not raised to it."

"You were born to it," said his aunt. "And that is enough."

"Is it? I wonder," mused Edmund.

"There is more than the sudden acquisition of

wealth and title that bothers you," guessed his aunt.

Edmund bit his lip and looked out the carriage window. "If I accept the present and the future then I must accept the past as well."

"It is Gerard isn't it?"

Edmund was silent, his throat too constricted to allow him to speak.

"Jonathan may have wished all the world to think otherwise, but you would not purposely have shot your brother," she said. "You loved him dearly. You would never have wished him harm."

"Not even if it meant inheriting a title?" responded Edmund cynically.

"If you wished the title, why did you not stay?" parried his aunt. "Besides, you were just a boy."

Edmund fell silent. Just a boy. Surely as a child he wouldn't be so heartless as to murder his own brother. He may have been a robber all these years, but he was not a cold-blooded murderer. Was he? "I wish I could give the curst title back," he said at last.

"I am sure Jonathan would be delighted to take it," said her ladyship scornfully.

Edmund fell silent. "I cannot help feeling sorry for the man," he said at last. "After all these years he must have felt quite safe in assuming it would be his to keep."

"If he did then he was a fool," said Lady Mary. "I told him at your brother's funeral I would never stop looking for you."

"Have you truly been looking for me all these years?"

Lady Mary nodded and looked out the carriage window. "I have had a man in my employ these past ten years whose sole job was to scour the countryside for you. As time passed all he had to go on was that birthmark at your temple. I must admit it came as a shock when he finally found you and through some discreet questions discovered what you had been up to these past few years."

"Then you knew who I was before I even robbed you," declared Edmund, amazed.

"I am not such a foolish old woman that I normally go haring about the countryside with no postillions." Her ladyship chuckled. "I am sure I looked like a ripe plum, indeed, to you," she said. "Bragging to the innkeeper of my bravery, and scoffing at his warning of highwaymen. Poor Susan. She had no idea what I was up to. I am sure she thought me mad. I never did explain to her the reason behind our strange traveling schedule. I suppose now that your claim has been proved I could do so."

"I am sure she would be amazed by your cleverness," said Edmund with a smile. "But it was a very dangerous chance to take."

Her ladyship smiled at him and her eyes filled with tears. "I had a great desire to meet you, you see. I am sure there are many who are scandalized by your past. But I am proud of you. You survived. Why you have no memory of who you are, why you never came to those who loved you when you were young I know not. I am only glad you are here now. And I know you will make me proud, Edmund."

Edmund took the old woman's hand and, kneeling at her feet, kissed it. Then, surprising both his aunt and himself, he buried his face in her lap and wept.

They arrived home to find Susan awaiting them in the drawing room, anxious to hear the outcome of the meeting with the duke and his lawyers. The whole amazing story was poured out for her— except the exact location of the telling birthmark— and she marveled and rejoiced with her aunt and the new duke.

"This is, indeed, an incredible story," she said at last. "But, Aunt, why did you not tell me?"

"I thought it best to tell no one until all had been proven," said her ladyship, again discreetly avoiding any mention of the final proof.

Susan turned to Edmund. "You must be very happy," she said kindly.

Edmund's face clouded. "I wish I knew exactly what I felt," he said. "My uncle did not take the news well."

Susan looked questioningly at her aunt.

"He worked himself into such a fit that he suffered a terrible attack," said Lady Mary. "You must stop blaming yourself for that," she told Edmund. "If we are to blame anyone, we must blame Jonathan himself for the debacle that occurred the day he took you boys out hunting. He should never have profited from such a misfortune, and the fact he is loath to see justice done speaks volumes about his character."

"As much as your nephew's concern speaks for his," said Susan, rewarding Edmund for his goodness with a smile.

"That is so," agreed her ladyship. "Now. Let us waste no more time mourning for my undeserving cousin, nor his son, for they will really suffer no great hardship because of this. The Wortleys have fortune enough on which to live very comfortably, and as happily ever after as we shall." She smiled at her nephew and sighed contentedly. "I do believe I could die tomorrow and be happy," she said.

"I shouldn't be happy at all if you were to do such a thing, so I pray you won't think of it," said Edmund.

"You will have me around to meddle in your affairs for some time yet, I fear," said her ladyship. Again, she sighed, this time from exhaustion. "This day's exertions have quite knocked me up. I think I shall go to my room and rest awhile."

Edmund walked with her to the door and the tender look he gave the old woman was not lost on Miss Susan Montague. "You have a kind heart, Edmund Morris Worthington," she said as he resumed his seat.

Edmund looked at her in surprise. "Why do you say that?" he asked.

Susan thought a moment. Her opinion of the new duke had been gradually changing in spite of her early determination to dislike him. Several small evidences of a kind heart sprang to mind: the way the interloper had moved to help the former duke when their first meeting brought on an apoplectic attack, the ridiculous story he had made up to keep secret his fight with his cousin, Jarvis, and then there was his loyal pride in the people who had found and raised him, and this strong bond that existed between him and his aunt. "The way you treat Aunt Mary is a fine example of kindness," she said. "You are very fond of her, aren't you?"

He smiled and nodded. "She is one of the two reasons why I remained in London."

"One? And what is the other reason?"

Edmund looked at Susan with a questioning smile. "Can you not guess, fair Susan?"

Susan blushed and lowered her eyes. "You seem to be very fond of Miss Ravenscort," she observed.

So we are to play a little game, eh? thought Edmund. Very well, I will play along. "Oh, I am," he agreed. A slight frown crossed Susan's face. "But she is not the reason I have remained," he continued, and had the satisfaction of seeing a smile of feminine triumph on Susan's lips.

If she had been a maid at the Blue Boar he'd have kissed her then and there, but he had learned that a saucy maid and a lady of gentle birth were two different animals and should be treated so. Besides, he and Miss Susan Montague had had their fair share of squabbles. He would wait awhile before laying all his newly-acquired earthly goods at her feet, just to be very sure she would not kick them aside, and kick him in the shins in the process! Instead of pulling her into his arms, he crossed one elegantly booted leg over the other and said casually, "I am sure now that my noble birth has been proved I shall be more acceptable as a husband."

Susan's heightened color told him all he needed to know. "I am sure that is so," she agreed and became suddenly occupied with draining the contents of her tea cup. "More tea?"

Edmund smiled at her. "I believe I should like another cup," he said politely and changed the subject.

The following day Edmund and the ladies had a morning caller. His cousin stiffly apologized for interrupting his breakfast.

" 'Tis no interruption," said Edmund cheerfully. "You may join us if you wish."

Jarvis shook his head. "No, thank you. I cannot stay long."

"How is your father?" asked Lady Mary.

"We have every hope for his recovery," said Jarvis. "In fact, that is why I have come." He turned to his new cousin. "Perhaps I might have a private word with you?"

"Of course," said Edmund, anxious to please. "In the library?"

Once in the library Jarvis did not waste time in idle chitchat. "My father would like to return one last time to Grayborough Hall. The doctors feel it would do his spirits good and speed his recovery. I would like your permission to take him there and stay with him." It was obviously hard for a man with Jarvis's pride to ask the new head of the family for such a favor. In fact, Jarvis's tone implied he meant to go whether he obtained his cousin's permission or not. A mean-spirited man would have denied him. Edmund was more than willing to forgive and forget. "Of course. Take him and stay as long as you please."

"Thank you," replied Jarvis, still stiff.

"And please convey to him our wishes for his speedy recovery."

"I am sure that will mean much to him as it was you who caused his illness in the first place," said Jarvis bitterly. "Good day, cousin."

Edmund watched him go. He could feel his blood simmering, bringing the angry flush to his cheeks, making his jaw lock and his fingers wish to clench. Let it go, he told himself. The fellow has a right to be angry. First he lost his expectations, now he is in danger of losing his father. Edmund sighed and, wondering if his cousin had even liked him as a child, returned to breakfast.

"You will never be rid of them now," predicted Lady Mary after hearing the purpose of Jarvis's call.

Edmund was not bothered by this. "They are my relations. Why shouldn't they stay at Grayborough Hall?"

"Because they have a perfectly good family home of their own to which they can, and should, repair," snapped Lady Mary.

"After so many years of stealing from my fellow man I should think you would be pleased to see me wishing to help him," said Edmund.

"The Wortleys are a havey-cavey lot," said her ladyship. "I don't trust 'em. You had best not either."

"I think it was very generous of Edmund to offer the use of the Hall," said Susan. "Most men in his position would not be so gracious." This kindness earned her a grateful smile from Edmund and a scowl from Lady Mary.

"And when will you be going there?" asked her ladyship.

Edmund shrugged. "As soon as London becomes 'thin of company.' That is the phrase, is it not?"

His aunt smiled. "How quickly you learn."

"I suppose I shall want to look in at the Blue Boar on my way," Edmund continued nonchalantly. Lady Mary rolled her eyes at this and her nephew shrugged. "I shall at least have to buy a mug of porter for everyone. It is only fair to share my good fortune with those who were so good to me for so long."

"And who taught you to steal and terrorize travellers," said Susan scornfully.

"Who fed me and clothed me and asked no questions about where I was from, who loved me for myself alone," countered Edmund hotly.

"Such people will love anyone, which shows you just what their love was worth," Susan retorted.

"They were good people, honest people. And they loved me in spite of the way I chose to earn my bread and butter!"

"Earn?" cried Susan, incensed. "I suppose you and your huge friend 'earned' my pearl necklace."

"Enough!" commanded Lady Mary. "Edmund, we have strayed far from the subject at hand.

When do you propose to move into the Hall?"

"July," said Edmund unenthusiastically.

"Jonathan will still be firmly ensconced when you arrive, mark my words," said her ladyship.

"Then I shan't be lonely," said Edmund, trying to sound cheerful.

Lady Mary nodded decisively. "Very well. If it is company you want, I am sure Susan and I would be delighted to be your houseguests."

Susan looked momentarily startled by such cavalier handling of her affairs, and even Edmund was a little surprised. But the thought of having the two most important women in his life at the Hall to help him settle in was a comforting one. He laughed good-naturedly. "I would, of course, be delighted to have you as my houseguests. I am always glad of your company. I sometimes wonder how glad our fair Susan is of mine." Edmund watched Susan as he spoke. "Are you ever glad of my presence, fair Susan?" he asked gently. *Are you still angry with me?*

She gave him a reluctant smile, then bowed her face. "I am afraid that, in spite of my better judgment, I do occasionally enjoy your company," she said.

Edmund grinned, sure that before his little house party in July had ended he and Miss Susan Montague would be betrothed.

9

THERE WAS MUCH tittering among the members of
the Upper Ten Thousand when the tale got out of
how Edmund Morris Worthington, the new Duke
of Grayborough, had proven his claim. And for
some, doubt still remained as to whether or not
he had satisfactorily proven it.

Edmund suspected his story had been made
common knowledge thanks to the efforts of his
cousin. A fine farewell gift, he thought irritably
as one gentleman at Boodles looked through him,
failing to return his greeting.

He shrugged mentally. It was only natural that
there would be some who felt the mere lucky
coincidence of possessing a birthmark should not
allow a lower-class usurper an entry into polite
society. And he realized that his inability to recognize trusted old retainers had made him look
very much like a usurper.

He was now sure he was the long lost Edmund Worthington. Little scenes were beginning

to emerge from the mists and stand out clearly in his mind: a boy—himself—in a pair of velvet nankeens, walking down a wide staircase; a pretty perfumed lady in a rustling gown bending over him to kiss him and calling him her darling baby; a long wall hung with a procession of portraits. Yes, he was Edmund. He knew it now. But there was much he still didn't know, many scenes hiding behind those swirling mists that refused to reveal themselves to him. So if he, who knew his true identity, was confused, why shouldn't the rest of society be?

His aunt was not happy with the continued refusal of some stubborn members of the ton to accept her nephew, and she said as much one morning at breakfast.

"It don't bother me," said Edmund, helping himself generously from the various chafing dishes on the sideboard.

"Well, it should. You are now the Duke of Grayborough, and these fools who are snubbing you ought to recognize the fact."

At that moment came the arrival of an invitation requesting the company of His Grace, the Duke of Grayborough, and Lady Mary Harriville and Miss Susan Montague at a ball to be given Saturday next by Lady Jersey. "Ha!" crowed her ladyship. "I see someone in this town has some sense after all, though I never thought Sally Jersey sensible."

"Queen Sarah herself, eh?" commented Edmund. "Does this mean I am to become socially acceptable to one and all?"

"It means the head of the committee of patronesses of Almack's means to do her best to make you so," said Susan. "How fortunate that she has such a kind heart. She can do you much good."

"Much I care," scoffed Edmund.

His aunt reprimanded him. "You should care, if not for yourself for your future bride and children."

Edmund was properly chastened by this remark and returned his attention to filling his plate with steak, eggs, and fish.

"Now we shall show the fools and tattlemongers a thing or two," declared Lady Mary, the light of battle in her eyes.

And, indeed, the night of the ball they did. Lady Jersey made a point of dancing with Edmund. Lady Cowper danced with him as well, and her husband, at his wife's bidding, made a point of speaking to the new duke. All the sporting-mad young gentlemen had never lost their high opinion of Edmund, and were as happy to see him established as duke as they were to talk with him.

No amount of proof could convince Countess Lieven, also a patroness of Almack's, that a former highwayman could possibly be a duke. But Edmund did not need her approval to ensure his social success. The blessing of Ladies Jersey and Cowper, Edmund's good nature, and the fact that his aunt was, after all, Lady Mary Harriville carried the day. And many, now that they came to think of it, realized that the former duke had been an ill-natured old fish, anyway. The new duke was handsome and amusing and anxious to please. He was also titled and wealthy. Oh, yes. A very delightful young man, indeed!

"Lady Cowper thinks you are charming," Susan informed him as he twirled her across the dance floor in a waltz.

"Does she?"

"You do not look properly impressed," observed Susan.

"There is only one person I want to think me charming," said Edmund, smiling down at her.

She blushed and smiled back. "Her husband thinks you very nice as well," she added.

"He thinks?"

Susan tried to look reprimanding and failed. "His lordship is a little dull," she admitted.

"Like this evening," muttered Edmund.

"You are not having a good time?"

"When I am dancing with you I am," replied Edmund. "But I must admit I am tired of making polite and witty conversation. I don't care if I ever again set foot in Almack's, and it would not break my heart if none of these society hostesses ever invited me to another ball. Who are these people, anyway, but a collection of spoiled, inbred, haughty fools?"

Susan stiffened. "I thank you kindly, sir," she said.

"Oh, not you. And not everyone. I rather like that Alvanley fellow, and Tommy Onslow. But really, these people give themselves such airs. And why? What is so wonderful about them?"

"Actually, I am not sure," admitted Susan. "I only know we were both born to their world. It is where we belong and where we must live. You especially, for you are a duke."

Edmund made a face.

"Is it so very terrible to be a duke?"

It was a gentle reproof, and Edmund smiled at the lovely girl in his arms. "No, I suppose not," he said. "After all, if I had not become a duke I would never have met you."

His partner rewarded this speech with a smile.

"Have I told you yet how beautiful you look tonight?" he murmured.

There was something in his tone which made Miss Susan Montague feel rather self-conscious, even a little nervous. She tried to make her tone light. "No. But now you have fulfilled your social obligation and done so you may feel free to talk of other things."

"There is nothing I would rather talk about than you," replied Edmund, smiling down at her. He lifted her hand to his lips and nibbled her fingers, causing a sensation which she found most alarmingly pleasant.

"Do try to behave yourself," she scolded.

"Are you scolding me because you consider kissing a beautiful woman's hands improper?" teased Edmund.

"You were not kissing. You were nibbling," corrected Susan.

A wicked grin grew on his face. "Yes, I was," he admitted. "And I find you more delicious than spun sugar. In fact, I have half a mind to dance you out onto the balcony and nibble that lovely shoulder."

Susan blushed. "You really should not say such things. It is most improper," she said. But her scold had lost its pepper and they both knew it.

"I suppose other men don't say such things to you," said Edmund.

"They certainly do not," said Susan, trying to sound proper.

"And do you not find them all a little dull?"

"Compared to a highwayman I suppose most men would seem a little dull," admitted Susan. Then, realizing the impropriety of such a confession, she scowled at him. "Oh, now look what you have tricked me into saying!"

He smiled at her and pulled her to him just long enough to whisper, "You are even more lovely when you pout."

Before she could make him a reply he swept her into a twirl that left her dizzy.

The music ended and he was about to suggest a stroll in the direction of the balcony when a young man came, claiming she was promised to him, and carried her away.

Edmund frowned and went in search of some diversion. He soon found himself among some young sporting bloods he had recognized from the Daffy Club, deep in a discussion of pugilism, and was unable to resist bragging about his new discovery. "I should like very much to see how this fellow of yours strips down," said one man.

"Oh, he wants training yet," admitted Edmund, thinking of James's footwork. "I am going to see if

I can get Tom Cribb to take him under his wing."

"He won't take just anyone," cautioned the man.

"He will take this one," Edmund predicted. "The fellow has the makings of a champion. He popped a good one in over my guard without even trying."

"Who is this champion and when will we be able to see him in action?" asked another man.

As Edmund was thinking on this another man spoke up. "I have a monkey that says it's all a hum and this fellow couldn't go two rounds with a real prizefighter."

"I'll wager a pony he could," said another.

"I know just the lad to take him," said yet another. "What is your boy's name?"

"James," replied Edmund. And, inspired, added, "Gentleman James."

"Gentleman James, is it?" scoffed the young man.

"You'd best beware, Carrington," teased a friend good-naturedly. "You know any fighter who puts Gentleman before his name is bound to be a champion. It certainly worked for Jackson."

Lord Carrington chuckled. "Well, my man is no gentleman, but John Armstrong never stays down. He'll be the next champion of England. I'd wager my title on it."

"I don't want your title. I just inherited one of my own," joked Edmund and the others laughed appreciatively. "But I will wager you a pony that my man can take your man, and with only three weeks training, too."

"Taken!" declared the young man.

Before any more fascinating details could be discussed about the upcoming mill, their hostess bore down on the young bucks and scattered them across the ballroom to do their duty and amuse the young ladies present.

Before separating, the boxing enthusiasts agreed to proceed on to Boodles after the ball for a friendly game of hazard and further discussion of the upcoming match between the two future champions of England.

Having been separated from his cronies, Edmund went in search of Susan. He found her free and led her onto the dance floor again.

Miss Montague's second dance with the Duke of Grayborough left her more dizzy than the first. Edmund had not spun nor twirled her, but he had managed to produce a much more unsettling feeling than any mere physical dizziness, for Miss Montague now felt herself slipping amidst a variety of emotions. In spite of her previous scoldings, she had found herself longing for Edmund to flatter her further, say more outrageous things to her, even to tempt her out onto the balcony and nibble her shoulder as he had threatened. But he had done none of those things. He had, in fact, seemed rather preoccupied. And now irritation with Edmund for having brought such unladylike thoughts out in her fought with irritation that he was no longer doing so.

Edmund was, indeed, a little preoccupied. Basking in the knowledge of Miss Montague's affection, he was, for the moment, content, and already spinning plans for the big boxing match. After the ball, he dutifully escorted his aunt and her charge home, and after bidding both ladies a fond goodnight, went on to while away what remained of the night hours in gambling and drinking.

"I believe my nephew is developing a great fondness for you," observed Lady Mary.

"I think, perhaps, he is merely being kind."

"Is it now considered an act of simple kindness to kiss a lady's fingers on the dance floor?" wondered her ladyship.

Susan flushed a deep red. "Your nephew is a shocking flirt," she stammered.

Her ladyship smiled. "I had a feeling you would come to love him," she said.

Susan sighed. "Oh, dear. I fear that is exactly what I am doing."

Edmund finally left the club when the first rosy lightening of the darkness declared the approach of dawn. His friends bid him stay a little longer, but he declared his luck out and himself ready for his bed. He left, whistling and thinking it wasn't such a bad thing, after all, to be a member of the Upper Ten Thousand.

He was no more than a street away from the club and about to hail a chair when a hoarse whisper and scuffling feet announced the presence of footpads. Edmund's heart took off at a gallop, and so did he, all the while cursing himself for a silly clunch. Here he was with no pistol, no swordstick, not even so much as a stick to hand.

One of his pursuers made a dive for him and caught him by the shoulders, taking him off balance and bringing him down. The two men struggled and Edmund was able to push his assailant off him, but in the process a sharp pain in his left shoulder told him the man had a knife.

Edmund scrambled to his feet only to be knocked down by yet another man. I'm done for, he thought. "Help!" he bellowed.

"Grayborough?" called a voice further down the street. Edmund heard the sound of running feet just before he saw the glint of the knife.

10

EDMUND ROLLED SIDEWAYS and his attacker's knife cut into his arm instead of delivering the mortal wound intended. The man swore and ran off after his friends.

"Grayborough! Are you all right, old fellow?" It was young Lord Carrington. He knelt beside Edmund and helped him sit up.

"Glad you happened by," Edmund said to his new friend. "It was nearly bellows to mend with me."

"These curst footpads. They get bolder all the time. Can you stand?"

Edmund nodded and his friend helped him to his feet. Shock coupled with his wounds made him sway.

"Here now! You are weak as a kitten," exclaimed his rescuer. "Worth has his carriage and we shall take you home in that. Can you make it back to the club?"

"If you will give me your arm, I believe I can," said Edmund, and the two made their way slowly back down the street.

There were many horrified exclamations at the sight of Edmund. What was it coming to when a fellow couldn't leave his club without being assaulted by strangers? Something definitely needed to be done about those footpads.

Edmund listened to the talk as his friends staunched his wounds, gave him claret, and bundled him into Lord Worth's carriage. He said nothing other than a heartfelt thanks for their kindness, but as the carriage made its progress through the streets of London to Grosvenor Square he mulled over what he was sure he had heard right before he had been set upon—"That's him!" Very picky, these footpads.

Edmund tried to keep both his return home and his condition a secret. But Harris, the guardian of the door, knew where his loyalties lay. Lady Mary was summoned immediately, and before James barely had his master's coat off, she was at his door demanding entrance to his room. Edmund moaned. "Go to bed, Aunt," he called weakly. "I am fine."

The door opened and Aunt Mary entered, her tall frame encased in a red velvet wrapper, her gray hair in curlpapers and covered with a lacy nightcap.

"Such a vision of loveliness," murmured her nephew, stretching himself out on his bed.

Lady Mary had paled considerably on seeing Edmund. She ignored his quip and rushed to his side. "What has happened? James, go for the doctor."

"There is no need," said Edmund. "They are both clean wounds and easily dressed, and if you will return to bed I shall rest much easier. I told Harris not to wake you."

"Harris is not in your employ," said her ladyship. She turned to James. "I shall need warm water, bandages, and basilicum powder."

James disappeared and Lady Mary returned her attention to her nephew. "What happened?"

"I was set upon by footpads coming home from the club," replied Edmund.

"Footpads, eh?" His aunt looked thoughtful. "Are you sure they were footpads?"

Edmund saw no sense in upsetting his aunt so he kept what he thought to himself. "Of course. What else could they be?"

Lady Mary sat regarding him and chewing her bottom lip. "You must have a care," she said. "Promise me there will be no more wandering the streets alone."

Edmund smiled at her. "I promise," he said.

He was up the next morning, stiff and hurting, but moving. He joined the ladies for breakfast and was rewarded for his efforts by the concern Susan showed for him. "Aunt has just told me about last night. How are you feeling?" she asked.

"I have felt better," he admitted.

"Does it hurt very much?"

Edmund smiled fondly at her. "If truth be told, yes. But just knowing you are concerned eases my pain considerably."

"No one woke me last night," said Susan, and looked accusingly at her aunt.

"And what good could you have done, my dear?" demanded her ladyship. "Better to let you get your rest. Anyway, you may help today by keeping the patient amused. I am sure there are a great many books in the library that Edmund has never had the opportunity to read."

"Should you like me to read to you?" asked Susan kindly.

Edmund assured her he would, and once in the library, insisted she sit close to him on the sofa so he could read over her shoulder. "For my reading skills are limited," he admitted. "Perhaps I can read along and improve myself."

Being so close to Susan, he found he had no desire to improve his reading skills. He found himself watching her as she read and inhaling the sweet fragrance of her hair. It smelled like roses, and he longed to unpin it and run his fingers through it.

Feeling his gaze on her, she looked up. "Edmund, you are not paying attention," she scolded.

"I am paying attention," he replied. "But not to the story." She looked at him sternly, and he sighed and leaned back against the sofa cushions. "I shall try to behave," he said. "Frankly, I am tired and sore enough that I have not the heart to misbehave."

"You must be feeling very poor, indeed," said Susan.

Edmund smiled. "You are very kind to entertain me. Please read on."

They passed a pleasant morning in this way. So pleasant, in fact, that they repeated the activity the following day. And the following. And the more time she spent in his presence, the more sure Miss Montague became that she was, indeed, falling in love with the roguish Edmund. Indeed, who could not love him? He was grateful for her every kindness. He had humor and a quick wit. And he had an uncanny knack for making her heart somersault. Although he did not kiss her, he always made sure of sitting thrillingly close when she read to him and murmuring in her ear.

Altogether, Edmund lost three days recovering from his wounds, and, pleasant as his invalidism had been, he was determined not to remain inactive a fourth. He had a fighter to train and much to do.

His first order of business, he decided, would be a move to the Grayborough townhouse so recently vacated by his relatives. There he knew he could train James without upsetting his aunt's entire household.

His wounds were extremely uncomfortable, but he managed to eat a breakfast large enough to convince Her Ladyship he was well on the way to recovery. "I am pleased to see you feeling better," she said.

"I am feeling much better," he replied. "And you will also be pleased to know that I am going to cease taking advantage of your hospitality and remove myself to the Grayborough town house," he announced. "Now that things are legally settled and my cousins have vacated, I think it is time I established residence there." He beamed on his breakfast companions. Did Susan look a little disappointed he was leaving?

Lady Mary's face fell noticeably but she recovered herself. "An excellent idea," she agreed. "I must say, we have grown accustomed to your presence and will miss you sorely."

"And two streets is a very great distance," added Edmund soberly.

His aunt smiled. "Rogue," she said.

"Does it seem odd to you that he is so suddenly set on moving into his own residence?" asked Susan later, as the two ladies sat embroidering.

"Of course it does," said her ladyship. "Naturally, as the new Duke of Grayborough it is only right and proper he take up residence in his own town house, but our Edmund is too much a social creature to voluntarily leave the companionship he has enjoyed here. He is up to something, I am sure."

Edmund was very busy the next few days, setting up his new establishment. At least, that is what he told his aunt. He omitted any mention of an excursion in the company of his valet to The King's Arms, at the corner of Duke Street and King Street, and a conversation with its owner, Thomas Cribb, champion heavyweight of England. Nor was there any mention of several visits made by master and servant to Jackson's boxing saloon.

He also failed to inform her ladyship of a little excursion far from the precincts of London, planned, unfortunately, for the same date as Lady Arnold's rout. "What do you mean you cannot go?" she demanded. "Susan and I look to you to escort us."

"I am sorry, but I cannot. I have important business which must carry me away."

Both his aunt and Susan looked at him suspiciously and he blushed.

"Never mind, Aunt," said Susan. "I am sure Lord Wentworth will be happy to escort us."

"That man-milliner!" exclaimed Edmund. "What would he be doing escorting you?"

"You have been rather busy of late," said Susan. "Lord Wentworth has been most kind and attentive."

"Oh, he has, has he? Well, you tell him if he gets too attentive I shall plant him a facer."

"Why don't you accompany us to the rout and tell him yourself?" suggested Susan.

"Because I have another previous engagement that I must keep," replied Edmund.

"Of course, if it is a previous engagement we can hardly expect you to break it on our account," said Susan reasonably. "I am sure Lord Wentworth will be able to see to our needs quite well. We are really most fortunate he has been so attentive."

"Lord Wentworth is becoming very particular in his attentions," put in Lady Mary. "I am sure we shall do fine without you."

Edmund suddenly found himself in a quandary. Susan was in danger of having her affections turned by a frippery fellow whom Edmund had met and disliked on sight. To lose Susan would be terrible. To lose her to a fop like Wentworth was unthinkable. But it was equally unthinkable to postpone James's upcoming match. No sporting gentleman in his right mind would do such a thing. Surely a duke had the right to attend a mill if he wished, and if the women in his life thought to make a lapdog out of him they could think again! "I am sorry," he said firmly, "but I cannot change my plans. I shall just have to leave you both in the capable hands of Lord Wentworth." And with that he took his leave.

"Do you think we were too hard on him?" asked Susan after he left.

Lady Mary shook her head. "He has been taking you far too much for granted of late. It cannot hurt to rattle him a little. After all, the season is nearly over, and I should hate to return you to your mama unbetrothed."

Susan had to admit she would hate to return to her mama in such a condition, but she had no desire to become engaged to Lord Wentworth, and she said as much to her aunt.

"Never fear," said her ladyship. "I am sure as soon as Edmund is done with whatever endeavor is so feverishly possessing him he will make his marriage proposal to you."

Edmund was making the very same resolve as he drove to his townhouse. Miss Montague could obviously not be trusted to keep from encouraging every rake and fop who came along, and the sooner he had her engaged to him the better. As soon as this mill was over he would settle that matter once and for all.

But in the meantime he had a fighter to train. James threw himself into the spirit of the thing, quickly culling knowledge from the variety of experts Edmund paraded through his days. The services of both the Gentleman and Mr. Tom Cribb, as well as some minor dignitaries from the world of boxing, were hired to turn James into "Gentleman James," the next champion of England, and all who worked with him had to agree he had the makings of a champion.

"He lacks science," said Mr. Jackson.

"Ah, but he is learning that quite rapidly," said Edmund optimistically.

"Yes, he is," agreed the Gentleman. "In a year's time, after he puts a few fights behind him I would be very much surprised if he did not make a real name for himself."

"Yes, yes," agreed Edmund. "But how would you say he will fare in two weeks?"

Mr. Jackson rubbed his chin. "I've seen Armstrong fight. Very good footwork. Great stamina, too, and there he has the advantage of your man. But in all other respects I should guess them to be equally matched."

And so it appeared, as the big day finally arrived and the two pugilists began their match outside St. Albans. Edmund had heavily promoted it, and the crowd was a large and roisterous one, filled with bucks and bruisers alike, each man calling encouragement to his favorite.

For a while it looked as if the valet turned prizefighter would, indeed, take his opponent. But partway through the fight James began to flag, and young John Armstrong, who had been already fighting and training a full year, took advantage of his opponent's lack of stamina. After nine rounds, James was down and Edmund and the other young man who had been acting as his second, couldn't bring him up to scratch. "Come on, old fellow," urged Edmund, trying to keep James standing on the mark in the dirt. "You have more bottom than this. One more round and I think we shall have him on the run."

"I am sorry, Your Grace," James panted, and fainted.

A cheer went up from the backers of John Armstrong, and Lord Carrington advanced to congratulate Edmund on the pluck his man had shown. "You say this is his first fight?"

Edmund threw a bucket of water in his fighter's face and James revived, spluttering. "That's the fellow," said Edmund. He turned to Lord Carrington. "Perhaps he needs a trifle more training," he admitted.

Lord Carrington nodded. "Footwork," he said.

Edmund reached a hand to James and pulled him to his feet. "Come on," he said. "Let's go to The Fighting Cocks and celebrate your first fight with a mug of porter." He turned to Carrington. "I'll buy you one as well and settle up with you."

"You'd best buy one for Worth and Searle as well," advised Lord Carrington, "for here they come to gloat."

The Fighting Cocks was already doing a bangup business when the gentlemen entered. They joined the masculine bustle and found a table. James hung back. "Well, come on now," said Edmund impatiently.

James shook his head. "I couldn't, your grace. It wouldn't be proper."

Edmund laughed. "Of course it would. Here are all these fellows dying to talk with a future champion, and you are worrying about form. Come and sit down."

The command issued, Edmund plunged deep into a discussion with a crony about the match, analyzing James's performance and making plans for his future.

James was about to join them when a tap on his shoulder distracted him. He turned around to find a short, middle-aged man with a large belly hovering at his elbow. "You showed yerself real well today," said the man.

"Thank you," said James and turned to join the others.

But the man's hand on his arm stopped him. "Allow me to introduce myself. Jem Johnston, former manager of Henry Pearce." James looked at him blankly. "The Game Chicken?" he prompted.

James nodded, as if he knew who The Game Chicken was.

"Yes," continued the man, "I've handled some great ones in my time. Ever see Jem Belcher fight?"

James shook his head.

"I had a hand in his training, too. Now, son, I'm looking for a new man to train, one who shows real bottom, one who's game enough to stay in there, not afraid to throw his heart over the rails. You look like such a man, my boy. You know, there's real blunt to be made in prizefighting. A promising young man like you could make his fortune, enough to buy a nice little inn like this and settle down. Got a sweetheart?"

James looked embarrassed by this question and raised his chin preparatory to a set-down.

"I thought so," said the man. "Handsome young fellow like you. Only stands to reason. Well, here's a way you could get the blunt to set yourself up in a snug little inn and marry that girl. As I said, you've got bottom. And you have what's needed to become a champion. I could tell from watching you, my boy. But what you need is someone to train you properly, not some nob what only does this as a hobby."

The man continued to talk, and the more he talked the wider James's eyes became. Soon James was nodding enthusiastically, and Edmund turned to see him talking with the little man as if they were old friends. "What's this?" called Edmund.

James seemed reluctant to speak in front of Edmund's friends. "If I could have a word with Your Grace outside?" he ventured.

Edmund looked puzzled, but left the taproom with his valet, the little man following at a discreet distance.

Once outside, James seemed at a loss for words. He cleared his throat nervously. "Well, go on, boy, tell him," prompted Mr. Johnston.

"If it is not too great an inconvenience, I should like to give my notice," squeaked James.

"Give your notice! It is a curst great inconvenience!" Edmund responded. "What of your fighting? And what of my neckcloths? And who is this fellow, anyway?" he finished irritably.

"Allow me to introduce myself, Yer Grace," said the man, bowing. "Jem Johnston, pugilistic expert and manager extraordinaire. I see in your boy the makings of a champion. And I should know, as it was none other than myself what coached Jem Belcher to fame, and Henry Pearce."

"The Game Chicken!" exclaimed Edmund in wonder. "You trained The Game Chicken!"

The man tried to look modest. "Among others," he said, then proceeded to name them.

Edmund turned to James. "This fellow could be a great help to you."

James nodded eagerly and waited for his master to consider.

It didn't take long. Edmund clapped him on the back and wished him luck. "If you should tire of having your eye blacked you have only to come to me," he added.

James was almost made incapable of speech by this overwhelming generosity. "Thank you, Your Grace," he managed.

Edmund shrugged. "Anyone can tie a neckcloth, but not everyone can become a champion boxer."

The little man whisked James away to a glorious future and Edmund returned to the taproom.

"But where is your man?" demanded Lord Carrington.

"Gone to make his fortune," said Edmund with a sigh.

"What?"

"That fellow who was with him just now, do you know who he is?"

Lord Carrington shook his head.

"None other than Jem Johnston," bragged Edmund, "interested in my boy."

"Who the devil is Jem Johnston?" asked Lord Carrington.

"Everyone knows who Jem Johnston is," said Edmund. Apparently, not everyone did know who Jem Johnston was, for everyone at the table looked at Edmund blankly. "He trained Henry Pearce and Tom Cribb," prompted Edmund. "And helped John Broughton lay down the rules of prizefighting."

"I went to see Tom Cribb four years ago, and I don't remember that fellow," said one man.

"Well, maybe this man worked with him before he became champion."

"And maybe this fellow is a braggart and a fraud and has stolen your man with promises of fame and fortune," suggested Carrington.

Edmund's brows knit. "No. You don't think so, do you?"

"He sounds like a fraud to me," put in another man.

Edmund swore and his friends laughed. "'Tis no laughing matter," he said. "Now I must go back to tying my own curst cravat."

"'Tis past time you learned to tie your own curst cravats, anyway," said Lord Carrington scornfully.

"I hear Wentworth's man is looking for a new position," said Lord Worth.

"No. Why?" asked Carrington.

"Wentworth ignored his advice on waistcoats," said Lord Worth and the other men guffawed.

Mention of that veritable tulip of the ton reminded Edmund that in nursing his fighter he had missed a certain rout the night before, and decided it did not behoove him to linger in St. Albans. He left his companions early and headed back to London, determined to get home, get a good night's rest, and put in a morning call to his aunt and her niece the following day.

It was a less than perfect Edmund who called at his aunt's townhouse that morning. The few specks of lint on his coat that had eluded him when he dressed himself were now obvious, and his cravat bore the marks of an amateur's hands. But he felt himself presentable enough. Until he was ushered into the drawing room and saw none other than Lord Wentworth himself ensconced in Edmund's favorite chair and looking crisp, clean, and perfect. Edmund frowned. "Wentworth, what are you doing here?"

Lord Wentworth greeted his rival with irritating complaisance. "Good to see you, Grayborough," he said casually. "It appears your man has been careless with your coat." He arose from his seat, stalking the lint on Edmund's jacket. "Allow me," he said, and picked off one of the offending pieces.

"Really, Wentworth," snapped Edmund, squirming away, "there is no need. You ain't a bloody valet."

Lord Wentworth rolled his eyes in Lady Mary's and Susan's direction. "Grayborough, the ladies," he cautioned in an undervoice. "Must watch the language, eh?" Only temporarily distracted, he now focused on Edmund's cravat. "I say, you must have been in a dreadful hurry this morning."

Edmund could see his lordship's hand itching to adjust his neckcloth and moved quickly out of range. "I was," he said. "I had urgent family matters to discuss with my aunt and Miss Montague."

Lord Wentworth took the hint. "Oh, certainly," he said. "I should be on my way." He bowed over the ladies' hands. "I shall look forward to driving with you this afternoon, Miss Montague, and to finishing our conversation." He turned to Edmund. "If you should like to let that man of yours go, I am sure my old valet would be an improvement. The fellow has become a little too puffed up for my tastes, but I am sure he would do you a great deal of good. He is, after all, an excellent fellow."

Why not? After all, Edmund needed a valet, and he had no desire to waste an entire morning interviewing for one. "Send him to me," he said. "As it happens I am suddenly in need of a valet."

Lord Wentworth was happy to oblige. "I am sure he will serve you well," he said. He turned to Lady Mary. "I find I need someone who will take direction and be guided by my tastes, but Masterson will be of infinite use to your nephew."

"It is very kind of you," replied her ladyship, trying not to smile at Edmund's insulted look. "I am sure the next time you see my nephew you will not recognize him."

"Oh yes, let us hope for that happy circumstance," agreed Lord Wentworth enthusiastically.

As Edmund was beginning to look apoplectic, Lady Mary hurried their guest from the room.

The door had no sooner shut than Susan began to giggle.

"Fop," muttered Edmund, seating himself. "I do think you may stop now," he told her. "It ain't that funny."

Susan tried to compose her features. "I am sorry," she said, and burst again into laughter.

"What has happened to James?" asked Lady Mary.

"James," repeated Edmund, stalling for time. "He has found another position." No sense boring the ladies with the details of James's sudden departure.

"I am sorry to hear that," said his unsuspecting aunt. "I had thought him quite devoted to you."

"Yes, well, he got a better offer and I urged him to take it," said Edmund. "No sense holding the fellow back."

"But surely as the Duke of Grayborough you could well afford to make him a higher offer than the one he received," pointed out her ladyship.

"Well, yes. I suppose I could have," said Edmund, scratching the back of his head nervously. "But 'tis done and that is that." Susan had finally stopped giggling and he turned to her and demanded to know what Wentworth was doing there.

"Paying a social call," replied Susan calmly. "He certainly has the right as he offered marriage to me only yesterday morning."

11

"MARRIAGE!" ROARED EDMUND. "Now, see here, Susan. You belong to me."

"Oh? And when did you propose marriage, Your Grace?" asked Susan sweetly.

"Why, well, I was going to," stammered Edmund. "As soon as I returned from St. Albans. Here now, we are not speaking of me. We were speaking of you. How could you accept such a, a . . . fop!" Edmund was up and pacing. "The fellow has no brain. And he probably hasn't the faintest idea how to kiss a woman properly. How could you possibly be happy with such a man?"

"I think this would be an appropriate time for me to excuse myself," said Lady Mary, rising. "I feel a sudden urgent need to speak with cook about tonight's dinner."

"What did you tell the fellow?" demanded Edmund, not noticing his aunt's departure.

Susan lowered her gaze demurely. "I told him

I needed one or two days to search my heart. I believe he expects me to give him an answer this afternoon."

"Well, you may send him a note this morning," said Edmund. "And if he needs any further proof of what lies in your heart he may come to Hyde Park and find you driving with me."

"But suppose I have searched my heart and find I cannot love a tyrant," said Susan.

Edmund's mouth fell open. "I? A tyrant?"

"You certainly have no right to act the jealous lover," she observed, "for you have made me no declaration."

"Then I shall now," said Edmund, and he fell on one knee in front of her. "I declare to you that there could be no other woman in all the world for me. I declare to you that there is nothing in this world I long to possess more than your high regard. And I declare to you that if you take Wentworth instead of me I shall strangle that fop with his own perfectly tied neckcloth." Susan smiled at this and he continued, "Fair Susan, I know I am rather a graceless fellow . . ."

"You are," agreed Susan, still smiling. "And you are a shocking flirt. You have taken me rather for granted, Your Grace, making overtures to me only when it pleased you."

"What!" exclaimed Edmund.

Susan held up a hand to silence him. "And while I will admit I have grown quite fond of you, I will also admit I find myself unwilling to give my hand and heart to a man who has treated me so casually."

"Casually!" Edmund jumped to his feet.

Susan nodded and looked at him accusingly. "Can you honestly say you have been constant in your attentions to me?"

Edmund was highly incensed. "For pity's sake, Susan. I have had a good many important things on my mind since I came to town. I had to prove my identity . . ."

"You had to train a prizefighter," continued Susan.

Again, Edmund's mouth dropped and his eyes bulged. "Where did you hear such a thing?"

"From Lord Carrington's cousin's sister. There were a number of invited guests missing from the rout—male guests."

Susan looked at Edmund with a mixture of triumph and reprimand and he found himself blushing. Curse the chit! This was no way to respond to a marriage proposal from a duke. She cared. She had just said as much. This behavior was ridiculous. "You cannot refuse me," he informed her. "I am, after all, Grayborough."

Susan laughed at this, further angering her haughty suitor. "Such conceit! You could be the Prince Regent and my answer would be the same."

This was the final straw. A million angry thoughts boiled so furiously in Edmund's mind he could not put any into words. With a red face and a frown he strode from the room. Susan watched him go and sighed.

Lady Mary returned to the room. "It would appear you have refused my nephew," she commented, taking a seat and taking up her fancy work.

Susan smiled unhappily. "I am afraid so."

"Then you are to become Lady Wentworth?"

Susan denied this with a mock shudder. "He has such a temper."

Lady Mary knew her protégée wasn't referring to Lord Wentworth. "I suppose he charged from the room before you were ever able to finish putting your thoughts into words."

Susan bit her lip and nodded. "It was not my intention to refuse him permanently."

"Here now, child. Don't cry."

Susan wiped away a tiny tear and gave her aunt a wobbly smile. "Oh, Aunt. You have been so good to me. And Mama expected so much from this season."

"And she will get it," said Lady Mary encouragingly. "Perhaps not before the season is over, but certainly before the year has ended. Do not forget, we go to Grayborough Hall the end of July, and many a house party has resulted in an engagement."

"I am afraid I mishandled him," confessed Susan. "And there is no other man I want. I should have accepted him."

"Nonsense. The boy needs a lesson or two in love. He has not seriously courted you. If he wants your hand let him earn it like a proper suitor."

"And what if he does not?" asked Susan.

"I think," answered her aunt confidently, "you may safely tell Lord Wentworth your heart is engaged elsewhere."

"Even if my future is not," said Susan miserably.

"It will be," Lady Mary assured her. "And if we cannot bring Edmund up to scratch I will give you another season, so there is nothing to worry about."

Nothing to worry about, indeed! Two marriage proposals thrown away in one day. Whatever would Mama say? And beyond that, whatever would Susan do? Lord Wentworth she could easily live without. But Edmund? Oh, he was a beast!

As if to punish her for her perfidy, Edmund did not appear at Lady Seeton's ball the following night. Lord Wentworth was no happier with her than Edmund and did not dance with her once. Susan found the evening to be very flat, indeed.

Edmund's evening was little better. He attended a cock fight, then proceeded to Boodles, where he imbibed a considerable amount of wine and lost an equally considerable amount of money. He returned to his valetless home, where he settled in the library and proceeded to drink himself to sleep. "Curst female," he muttered as he slipped into unconsciousness.

It was the following day when Lord Wentworth's former valet, Masterson, presented himself to offer his services to His Grace, the Duke of Grayborough, and was shown to the library, where he found His Grace sprawled in a chair.

Masterson blanched at the sight of his future employer. The duke regarded him through bleary eyes. He appeared to have at least two days' growth of beard forming on his chin. And what was that mark on his face? Masterson's horrified gaze travelled downward to the desecrated neck-cloth and the waistcoat with the large wine stain and the stocking with the tear.

Edmund rubbed his forehead. "What time is it?" he mumbled.

"Two o'clock in the afternoon, Your Grace," replied Masterson politely.

Edmund rubbed his entire face, sending the hairs in his eyebrows in a variety of directions and making himself look like a satyr. He moaned. "Let me find my bed and sleep for another two hours. My head aches like the devil. If, when I wake, you can make me presentable you may consider yourself employed."

"Very good, Your Grace," agreed Masterson, rising to the challenge. "I shall return at four o'clock."

Edmund yawned noisily. "No need bothering to leave. Go on to the kitchen and have cook give you some cold mutton and some porter or a cup of tea, or whatever it is valets like to eat this time of day." With a moan Edmund staggered off to his bedroom and sought slumber to hide from his troubles a little longer.

At four o'clock Masterson was back and Edmund was politely but ruthlessly dragged from his hiding place. Before he knew what had happened he was washed and shaved. He was dressed and his cravat expertly tied. Except for the red eyes, a very fine-looking gentleman stared back at Edmund from his looking glass and he was well pleased. He gave his neckcloth a little tug and heard a gasp behind him.

"Do be careful, Your Grace," pleaded Masterson.

"Oh, sorry," mumbled Edmund. He turned and clapped the surprised valet on the back. "Well, old fellow, you have done a bangup job on me. Slap up to the nines. You will do very nicely."

"Thank you, Your Grace," murmured Masterson, flattered.

"And whatever Wentworth was paying you I shall double. I shall probably be twice as much work."

"Thank you, Your Grace," said Masterson, turning pink with pleasure.

Edmund left the capable hands of his new valet and decided to take a stroll. On Bond Street he met none other than that veritable tulip of the ton, Lord Wentworth. "I say, is that you, Grayborough? You do look smashing!" approved his lordship.

"I have hired your old valet," Edmund informed him.

Wentworth looked enviously at Edmund's flawless ensemble. "No one is better than Masterson," he said.

"How is your new man working out?" asked Edmund.

"Oh fine, fine. He has not quite Masterson's touch, you know, but I shall soon have him properly trained."

"And how was your drive with Miss Montague?" asked Edmund innocently.

A delicate pink inflamed his lordship's fair skin, but he shrugged. "Oh, it was a very nice drive. A very nice girl, don't ye know, but not for me, I think. Not enough interest in fashion."

She turned him down, thought Edmund gleefully as he parted ways with Lord Wentworth. Well, I knew she would. 'Tis me she wants. I should send her a little something to reward her for her wise decision.

Later that day a basket of hothouse strawberries arrived at Lady Mary's townhouse for Susan, along with a note which said, "In appreciation of your excellent taste." She read the note and smiled. How sweet! So he is going to court me, after all. But whatever could be the meaning of this note?

Later that night at a small dinner party given by his aunt, Edmund found himself seated next to Susan, who thanked him for his lovely present. "They are most delicious," she said.

"I am glad you liked them," said Edmund.

"It was kind of you to think of me," said Susan politely.

"I am always thinking of you," he replied.

"I would never know that if I were to judge by your behavior," she said. Edmund frowned and she smiled teasingly at him. "But I am glad to see you are changing your ways," she said encouragingly.

"Changing my ways?" inquired Edmund.

"Why, yes. Your present this morning . . ."

"Not my present," corrected Edmund, "your reward."

"Reward?"

"You did turn down Wentworth, did you not?" he whispered.

Susan blushed. "I am sure my conversation with Lord Wentworth can be of no interest to you," she replied crossly.

A great, self-satisfied smile grew on Edmund's face and he attempted to cover her hand with his. This was probably not a wise move, as her fingers were curled around her wine glass at the time. "Will you please try for a modicum of proper behavior," she hissed, and jerked her hand free, spilling wine on the table cloth as well as Edmund's jacket. She blushed fiercely and turned to the matron on her other side, visiting determinedly with her for the remainder of the meal.

The woman, who had seen poor Miss Montague's predicament, supported her by giving the young lady her undivided attention and preventing that young rogue from upsetting her any further.

Edmund glared at his turbot and determined to leave London the following week.

Later that evening, Masterson examined the sleeve of his master's jacket with strong disapproval, and Edmund, feeling like a boy caught stealing apples, found himself apologizing and trying to explain to his valet how he had come to be so careless with his clothes.

"Wine is very difficult to get out," reproved Masterson. "I shall try, but I cannot guarantee success," he finished, shaking his head.

"Ah, well," said Edmund philosophically. "We shall be leaving for the country next week. If the stain remains I shall wear it there."

The thought of his master wearing a stained

jacket even at home was a horrible one. "But Your Grace, if someone were to call unexpectedly?"

"All right, then. You may have it."

Masterson was obviously horrified at the thought.

Edmund looked at his valet in irritation. "Well, what the devil do you expect me to do, then."

"If the stain cannot be got out, I am afraid—"

"If the bloody stain won't come out, throw the bloody jacket away. For heaven's sake, man. I don't care what the devil you do with the thing. Just don't trouble me about it!"

"Yes, Your Grace," replied Masterson with a wounded sniff.

Oh, now he had hurt the fellow's feelings. What a bother servants were! Edmund found himself wondering where James was and how his prizefighting career was coming.

The following week Edmund took his leave of London, his aunt, and the fair Susan. He managed to steal a kiss from Susan, for which he got his ears soundly boxed and was sent on his way with the information that he was a conceited, ill-mannered, horrid creature.

"I shall miss you, too, love," he had called sweetly from the door and left before the red-faced young lady on the drawing room sofa could think of any new epithets to hurl at him.

He had made one other important call before leaving town, and that had been to Rundell and Bridge, where he had selected an expensive trifle with which to surprise Susan when she came to the Hall to visit.

Now as he made his way to his ancestral home, via the Blue Boar, confident of Susan's love, his future stretched before him like a golden highway. Life was, indeed, very good for Edmund Morris Worthington, Duke of Grayborough, who was blissfully unaware that there were those who would as soon see that good life come to a quick end.

12

EDMUND JUMPED FROM his horse and ran up the steps of the Blue Boar, shouting for the innkeeper.

The first person he encountered was a petite young woman with a round face, freckles, and golden curls. She was carrying a mop bucket and a scrub brush and she dropped both at the sight of Edmund. "Dickie!" she squealed and ran into his open arms.

"Mary, my girl!" he cried and spun her around. "Let me look at you," he said and set her down. "You are prettier than ever."

The girl blushed. "Oh, pooh," she laughed.

"And where is that big lout, Samson? Has he proposed marriage to you yet?"

Again the girl blushed, this time with obvious guilt. "He said you wasn't comin' back no more," she said. "Told us all you'd gone off to be a fine gentleman." She looked wonderingly at Edmund's clothes and the finely-dressed man

137

standing behind him. "And I guess you have," she added with awe.

"I have," admitted Edmund. "But I've come back to visit my old friends and buy a mug of porter for every man in town, so you may spread the word."

"I must find Samson," said Mary, and leaving her mop bucket forgotten in the entryway, she rushed from the inn.

"What's all this commotion?" demanded a deep voice from down the hall. "Mary, is there someone here? Mary!"

"There is, indeed, someone here," called Edmund. "And I wish a room, and be quick about it!"

A thin little man, ill matched to his big voice, came bustling down the hall. "A thousand apologies," he began. "I hope Your Lordship hasn't been waiting too long. I—" He stopped and stared at Edmund.

"Well, what is it?" demanded Edmund imperiously.

"Oh, nothing, Your Lordship. It is just that—"

"It is not Your Lordship," corrected Edmund. "It is Your Grace, for I am a duke now." He struck a pose and then began to laugh. The man smiled hesitantly, still obviously confused, and Edmund laughed more heartily. He clapped the older man on the back and gave him a one-armed hug. "Come now, Jonsey, don't you recognize your adopted son?"

"Lord bless us!" exclaimed the man. " 'Tis Dickie!" His eyes filled with tears and he hugged Edmund. "Dickie boy, Dickie boy. We never thought to see you again. And won't Mother be surprised! I hope she don't die of fright when she sets eyes on you."

The man turned and ran down the hall, leaving Edmund and his servant standing in the entryway. Masterson let out a pained sigh.

Five minutes later Mr. Jones, proud owner of the Blue Boar, had returned with his disbelieving wife in tow. At the sight of Edmund she clapped both plump hands to her cheeks. "Lord love us, 'tis our own Dickie!" she cried, and ran to him and threw both arms round his neck.

"Mother Jones," he whispered, and hugged her.

"Let me look at you," she commanded. "Mercy! What a fine gentleman you turned out to be. Who'd ha' believed our own Dickie boy was really a duke. Oh, but look at you. Hot and tired, no doubt. Father, find our boy a mug of porter. Oh, and his friend, too," she added, smiling at Masterson. "And rooms! I am sure Dickie will want to wash. And you come on back to the kitchen when you're done. I am going to make you a strawberry tart."

Royalty never had a better reception than Edmund received from his old friends. He sent Masterson off to play with his clothes and spent the afternoon in the kitchen visiting with Mrs. Jones, sampling her baking, and flirting with the maids. His old friend Samson joined him and, like the others, marveled at his transformation. " 'Tis a good lay, eh?" he asked. "If anybody could bring off such a trick you could, Dickie boy."

"It is no trick, old friend," said Edmund. "I am, in truth, Grayborough." And he proceeded to tell his adopted mother and his best friend the mysterious story of his childhood.

Samson whistled. "But you don't remember none of this, eh?"

Edmund shrugged. "I remember bits and pieces."

"And how does the old duke like all this?"

"Oh, he is as mad as a wet hen," admitted Edmund. "In fact, I was set upon by some of those bloody footpads we used to hear about—nasty cowardly fellows—and for a while I thought his son, my cousin Jarvis, had set them upon me." Edmund shrugged. "But perhaps I was mistaken."

"And perhaps not," said Samson. "This fellow Jarvis, did you say he would be the next duke if you hadn't come along?"

Edmund nodded. "He likes me no more than his father."

Samson nodded thoughtfully. "Where are these coves now?"

"They are at Grayborough Hall, enjoying my hospitality," replied Edmund.

Samson frowned. "Don't they have no home of their own?"

"Oh yes," said Edmund cheerfully. "It so happens they like mine better."

Samson rolled his eyes. "I never thought I'd live to hear myself say it, but I am glad I ain't a nob."

Edmund sighed. "Sometimes I wish I weren't." Then he thought of Susan. "But it does have its advantages," he finished cheerfully. "I do miss your cooking, though," he said to Mrs. Jones. "Nobody can make a strawberry tart that compares with yours."

This compliment earned him another helping and an insistent invitation to stay at the Blue Boar for as long as it suited him.

It suited Edmund to stay for a month, during which time he teased the maids, accompanied Samson on one or two robberies for old times' sake, attended several local mills and cock fights, and swapped stories with the locals over large, constantly replenished mugs of porter.

But finally he could delay his return to the ancestral home no longer. "We leave tomorrow," he informed Masterson.

His valet had not enjoyed their sojourn at the Blue Boar, finding himself much above fraternizing with the locals. His employer's familiarity with such common people had shocked him, and the duke's casual interest in his clothing was, to Masterson's way of thinking, equally improper. Unbeknownst to Edmund, Masterson had only the day before written a letter to Lord Wentworth, relaying his horrible working conditions, and offering his services to the earl should his present valet prove unsatisfactory. He received Edmund's news with hope that things would possibly improve when they reached their next destination and the stronger hope that he would hear soon from Lord Wentworth. Masterson had his grace properly decked out the following morning and found, now he was leaving, he could look on the inhabitants of the environs of the Blue Boar with equanimity and tolerance. He smiled down from his perch high atop the duke's curricle on a world and people he would, thankfully, never see again. And his smile remained, even when Samson came up alongside them on his huge black horse.

"Are you sure you would rather not stay here?" asked Edmund.

Masterson's smile began to fade.

Samson nodded. "I got a fancy to see how the nobs live," he said.

"Well, and so you shall," said Edmund. "I am sure you will make a much more entertaining houseguest than my sour-faced relatives."

"Houseguest?" repeated Masterson.

"Yes," said Edmund cheerfully. "You won't mind giving old Samson's grimy neckcloth an occasional twist, will you, old fellow?"

"No, Your Grace," replied Masterson faintly. "Meaning no disrespect, Your Grace, but does Mr. Smythe own any neckcloths?"

Edmund looked down his nose at his friend. "My valet wishes to know if you own any neckcloths," he said.

"Of course I own neckcloths," said Samson, insulted. "And I still have the coat and waistcoat we took off that fat cove last September."

Edmund turned to his valet. "Mr. Smythe assures me he has neckcloths. May he come along?"

Masterson flushed deep scarlet. "I am sure it pleases Your Grace to jest," he said stiffly.

Edmund grinned, slapped the horses' reins, and called a cheery farewell to the friends who had come out to see him off.

"You behave yourself, now," Mary called to Samson. "And remember you are in a gentleman's house!"

"Gentleman's house!" exclaimed Samson later that day at the sight of Grayborough Hall in all its huge and rambling glory. " 'Tis a king's castle, more like."

Edmund made no reply. He had been lost in thought, chasing illusive images through the mist.

The household had been alerted as to their arrival and Ames, the butler, met them at the door. His eyes widened fractionally, and only for a moment, at the sight of Edmund's large, common-looking companion before he calmly informed His Grace how happy they all were to receive him. The rest of the servants were assembled and waiting to make their bow or curtsy to the long-lost heir. Edmund's aunt would have been proud to see how well he performed his duty, giving a kind word to each member of his staff, displaying the newly-donned dignity that his position required.

But he found it hard to maintain that dignity when he and Samson entered the library and the presence of the former duke and his son. For someone presumed to be at death's door, his cousin looked hale and hearty, and Edmund felt himself flushing like a guilty little boy and stammering a greeting and introduction.

"Hello, Your Gra . . . , Lord . . . er, ahem." Samson cleared his throat and made a clumsy bow.

The former duke reduced to an earl looked past the large man, choosing to ignore his existence completely. He smiled benignly on his cousin and welcomed him to his rightful home.

Edmund felt suddenly very uncomfortable, more like an interloper than the master. Neither Jonathan nor Jarvis had risen to greet him and neither had offered him a seat. He stood, feeling gauche and uncomfortable. "I am glad to see you recovered," he ventured.

"I am feeling much better, thank you," said the older man. His smile was a challenge. "We have enjoyed your hospitality these past two months," he said. "I am sure now you are here you would as soon be rid of your old cousin."

"Oh, no," insisted Edmund, anxious to please, yet cursing himself for a coward. "I hope you both will stay as long as you like."

"Thank you," said Jarvis coldly.

"Very good of you, my boy," said the former duke condescendingly. "Feel free to explore. We do not keep town hours. Dinner is at five."

He had been dismissed. The Duke of Grayborough had been dismissed from his own library! Edmund left the room, the flabbergasted Samson behind him. "Are you goin' to let that little ant do that to you?" he demanded.

"Going to? I believe I already have." Edmund ran a hand through his hair and sighed.

Samson shook his head in disgust. "Never thought I'd see the day when Dickie White would let another man push him about like he was in petticoats."

Edmund took a turn about the hall. "I believe I saw a decanter of some of *my* wine in the library. Do you feel like a drink?"

"That's the thing!" said Samson encouragingly and followed his friend back into the library.

The earl and his son looked up in surprise as Edmund and the large man reentered the room. "Yes?" said Jonathan.

"I find traveling to be very thirsty work. I think Samson and I will have a drink and enjoy my library a while. If you have no objections, that is." Edmund did not wait to hear any objections, but turned to the decanter and filled two glasses.

The library was a large room, at least seventy feet long, and besides a good collection of books, contained a variety of other amusements: a drawing table, a billiard table, and several good paintings. Sofas and chairs were scattered about the room, and for the daydreamer a bay window offered a view of the pleasure garden. Edmund wandered over to the window and surveyed his domain, trying to ignore the incensed stare of two pairs of eyes boring into his back.

Samson dropped into a chair and slung a beefy leg over its arm. There was a slight gasp at the other end of the room and he raised his glass in salute to the other two men.

"Perhaps a stroll in the garden would be good for you, Father," suggested Jarvis.

"Yes, quite," agreed the earl, and they left the room without a word to their host.

The door shut and Samson guffawed. "That ought to send 'em back where they come from."

But Edmund's relations were made of sterner stuff. Jarvis paid Edmund a visit in his bedroom before dinner. "I wish you would be plain with me," he said without preamble. "Do you wish us to leave?"

"Your father makes me curst uncomfortable," admitted Edmund. "But this has been his home for many years. I have no desire to drive him from it."

Jarvis nodded. "My father is much improved, but a sudden removal would most likely not be good for him."

"Then he must stay as long as he wishes," said Edmund.

Jarvis said a cold thank-you which obviously cost his pride greatly and left.

" 'Tis a cold fish, that one," said Samson, who had been lounging nearby, watching Masterson at work.

"The fellow hates me," said Edmund. "But I suppose I should hate me, too, if I were in his boots."

"I think he'd as soon slit your gullet as not," observed Samson.

Edmund shrugged. "The nobs don't go around cutting each other's throats," he said.

"They ain't that honest. So if I was you," said Samson, "I'd watch my back."

13

DURING THE FOLLOWING week Edmund's relations treated him and his friend like lepers. They avoided the duke and his low friend throughout the day, either keeping to their rooms or hiding in the library. When the usurpers entered the library the Wortleys went outside. If Edmund and Samson fancied a stroll, or mentioned fishing in the stream, Jarvis and his father remained indoors. Only the necessary taking of meals was done together, and even during that time father and son always managed to carry on a conversation that excluded their host. For such a large establishment, it was amazing how small it had become. Everywhere Edmund went he encountered his cousins avoiding him, and Edmund, who had always prided himself on being able to get along with his fellow man, felt the snubs sorely. His only consolation was in the letter he received from his aunt, announcing her intended arrival the following week.

The day he received the news he was cheered so much that, in spite of a chilly reception at dinner, he felt so in charity with his cousins as to challenge them to a game of billiards.

"You never cease to amaze me, cousin," said Jarvis. "Do you mean to tell me that in your colorful past you also found time to master billiards?"

Edmund raised his chin haughtily. "I do not mean to tell you any such thing. But I do believe a friendly game would do much to while away the evening hours. And I am sure it would please my aunt and her niece to arrive next week and not find us at daggers drawn," he added, playing his trump card.

Jarvis sighed. "As you wish," he said, rising.

Edmund and Samson followed the other two men into the library, Samson looking at his friend as if to ask, "Are you crazy?" Edmund merely shrugged.

"Does Mr. Smythe play?" asked Jarvis, politely taunting.

"I'll watch," said Samson.

"Pour us some port, then, old fellow," suggested Edmund.

His cousin racked the balls and, with a flourish of the arm, offered Edmund the chance of breaking them.

Edmund had never played billiards in his life. "After you," he said.

Jarvis nodded and broke the balls. Edmund watched as he played, taking note of how he held the cue stick. He allowed Jonathan to go next and observed him, as well. He shot and missed. "Father, are you deliberately making it easy for our cousin?" teased Jarvis. "Here's a shot you'll not likely miss," he said to Edmund.

It looked easy enough. The cue ball and the colored ball were perfectly aligned. Edmund balanced the cue stick between his fingers in a good imitation of his cousin and gave a mighty shove. The stick slid from his fingers and dove, with a ripping noise, along the table. He looked at the ripped cloth in dismay.

"Perhaps this isn't your game," suggested Jarvis. He turned to the earl. "Would you care for a game of piquet, Father?"

Edmund watched them repair to a corner of the library and ground his teeth. "I'll have a drink of that port," he said.

"May as well play a hand or two, ourselves," said Samson, trying to sound cheerful.

Edmund drained his glass and poured himself another.

The ormolu clock on the mantelpiece ticked the hours away as the two pairs of gentlemen sat in their respective corners of the library playing at cards, the one pair playing quietly, the other becoming increasingly more raucous.

The Wortleys finally admitted defeat and left. "I'd say the air has just got a bit cleaner-smelling in here," said Samson as the door closed.

Edmund chuckled, sure his high-in-the-instep cousins had heard and been properly insulted.

"Why don't you give 'em the boot and be done with it?" suggested Samson.

"How the devil can I do that? They're my relatives."

Samson was not impressed with this argument. "Simple as pie. You say, 'I've had a belly full of you both. Get yer bones out of my house.' Faugh," he said in disgust. "A fine pair of gentlemen they are. If that's wot the nobs are like I'd as lief stay wot I am. Should have shoved that funny little stick down the fellow's gullet," he muttered.

Edmund chuckled and rang for the butler. "Bring us another bottle or two of port," he said. "Drinking is something I know how to do," he told his friend.

"Ha!" scoffed Samson. "You wasn't never no good at that."

"Think you so?" Edmund poured two glasses of wine. "Let's just see."

The two men drank steadily for two hours, entertaining themselves with ribald jokes and songs, enjoying reminiscences of their days together as highwaymen, until Edmund's eyelids began to droop.

"See? I said you was a poor excuse for a drinkin' man. The stuff always used to knock you out better 'n a uppercut to the jaw."

Edmund waggled his head. "Nah. It takes more than a few glasses of wine to get me foxed."

"Foxed? You passed that long ago. Yer drunker 'n a lord."

"Course I am," snickered Edmund. "I'm a duke."

The two men laughed uproariously. Edmund finally turned serious. "Now. Where were we?"

"Freddy Fingers," said Samson.

"Ah, yes. As I was saying . . ." Edmund squinted at the two Samsons, trying to pull them back into one. "July fourteenth. That's the day they hung him. I remember cause somebody said it was the same day that French place was stormed."

Samson shook his head. "Well, they was wrong, and so are you. It was in August. August fourteenth. I remember cause it was my sister's birthday, and I was s'posed to bring her back somethin' from . . . Lunnen. And I forgot." Samson shook his head, looking much like a great shaggy dog shaking off water, and took another drink from his glass. "And that's all there is to it," he finished, shaking a drunken finger at his friend.

"Well," said Edmund doubtfully, "if you're sure."

"Course I'm sure. You think I don't know when my own sister's birthday is?"

"I guess a fellow ought to know that," conceded Edmund. "I'm going to bed."

Samson chuckled. "Told you you couldn't hold yer wine," he said, and stumbled out of the library after his friend. "Oh, I'm in love with the innkeeper's daughter," he began to sing.

Edmund joined him and they made their way to their respective bedrooms, giving the unwanted houseguests an off-key serenade.

Edmund collapsed onto his bed and promptly began to snore.

Samson, however, was still wide awake. He pulled off his boots and flopped onto his bed with a deck of cards to entertain himself at soli-

taire. An hour passed. "Maybe the runt is right,"
said Samson thoughtfully. He scratched his head.
"When was my sister's birthday?" He sat, staring
at the cards and cogitating. Finally, he slapped
his knee. "It is July fourteenth! Well, wot do you
know?"

Of course, Edmund would have happily waited
till morning to hear that he had, indeed, been
correct about the date of Freddy Fingers' demise.
But his friend wasn't one to put off till tomorrow
what could be done tonight, even if it was so late
it had already become tomorrow. Samson hoisted
his bulk from the bed and, grabbing his candle,
padded out of the room into the hallway. He
sniffed. What was that smell? Smoke! Samson
broke into a run.

Feathers of smoke were drifting out from under
Edmund's door. Candle still in hand, Samson
crashed into it and sent it flying open. Once inside
the room he was plunged into a fog of smoke.
The candle dropped, forgotten, and the big man
coughed and grabbed at his throat. Instinctively,
he ran to the bed and pulled the inert figure from
it. He slung his friend over his shoulder and ran
from the room. "Fire!" he croaked.

A figure in a brocade dressing gown appeared
at his side.

"Get help," coughed Samson.

Jarvis was already gone, and Samson hurried
back to his room with Edmund. He threw his
friend on the bed and, not knowing what else to
do, grabbed his water pitcher and emptied its contents in the duke's face. Nothing. Samson blinked

and shook his head. "Oh, no," he said. "No cold cock is gonna get you yet, Runt." He slapped Edmund's face. But there was no drunken smile, no response at all. "Breathe, blast you! Or I'll blow the breath of life into you meself!" The big man's voice broke, and between sobs, he did the desperate thing he had threatened. He covered his friend's mouth with his and blew.

There was a shuddering. Eyes fluttered. Edmund stirred.

Samson stared at his friend. "My Gawd," he said reverently. "It worked."

Edmund rewarded his friend's unorthodox rescue by vomiting on his bed. He moaned and fell back, holding his head.

"Yer house is burning," said Samson conversationally.

14

EDMUND'S EYES WIDENED and he struggled to get up.

"Stay here," said Samson and returned to the hallway. Servants were rushing about with buckets of water, Jarvis supervising. The earl was up now, too. Everything was well in hand. He returned to his room. "Looks like the nobs got it under control," he reported. "Didn't think that cousin of yours'd want to see the place go up in smoke." He flopped into a chair. "How'd you manage to set yer room on fire?"

"I don't know," said Edmund. "I don't remember anything. I don't even remember going to bed."

Samson shook his head in disgust. "You've got a poor head for wine, Dickie boy."

"I'm lucky I've got a head left at all," said Edmund. "Or a body. I could have been burned to a cinder if not for you. Thanks, old fellow."

Samson shrugged off the thanks in embarrass-

ment. He studied his friend. "If you didn't do anything, how do you think that glimmer started?"

Edmund sighed wearily. "How should I know?
Perhaps a spark from the fire landed on the rug."

"Was there a fire in your hearth?"

"I don't know. I didn't notice. It was a little
chilly this evening. There could have been."

Samson shook his head. "I spy the cloven foot
in this business, Dickie boy. I think someone set
a fire in your room after you went to bed. They
knew we had a pretty batch of it. Any cull could
peek in here and see you was clear. And who do
you think I saw out in the hallway when I was
carryin' you out?"

"Who?"

"None other than your high-and-mighty cousin,
Jarvis, that's who. Wot was he doin' tippy-toein'
about, I wonder?"

Edmund rubbed his forehead. "This is a fine fix.
Here I am, with my aunt and Susan due to arrive
in just a few days, and this happens."

Samson grunted.

"Well, we have a few days. Mayhap we can
repair the damage before they arrive and none
the wiser," said Edmund optimistically.

"The sooner they get here the better, I say," said
Samson. "Maybe, with more people in the place,
that cousin of yers will think twice before tryin'
to put an end to you."

Edmund didn't reply. He was asleep.

The next morning he woke with a headache,
which didn't improve with the resignation of his
valet. Masterson had had all he could endure. It

had been bad enough being valet to a gentleman who had no desire to be a gentleman. But, he informed the butler, he would not remain to be burned in his bed. He planned on leaving for Lord Wentworth's country seat that very day in the hopes that if he threw himself upon his former employer's mercy, he would be taken back.

"Well, he was a fussy old maid, anyway," Edmund said to Samson. "Tying a cravat and giving a fellow a shave ain't that hard. I'll have no trouble replacing him."

Seeing his charred room was not as easy to shrug off. "Feel like givin' the nobs the boot now?" inquired Samson.

"Edmund, my boy," Jonathan greeted him at breakfast. "Good to see you are still with us. Pity about the room."

Edmund said nothing, but went to the sideboard in search of sustenance. He did, indeed, feel like giving his cousins the boot, but he couldn't bring himself to do it. A fine fellow he should look, turning his relatives out the minute he got the title. That one would go down well when the ton heard of it.

Cleanup operations were well under way by early afternoon when Lady Mary and her niece arrived, but the acrid smell of smoke still lingered in the great house. Greetings were barely exchanged before Lady Mary sniffed and demanded, "What is that horrible smell? Has something burned?"

"Just a little accident," said Edmund lightly. Samson fidgeted next to him, dying to tell all, but afraid to speak in such elevated company. Edmund quieted him with a subtle elbow jab to the ribcage. "This is a pleasant surprise," he said, taking his aunt by the elbow and propelling her into the drawing room. "We did not expect you till next week."

But his aunt was not to be so easily distracted. As soon as they were settled she brought them back to the subject of the fire.

"It was a terrible thing," said the earl. "A spark from the hearth caught the rug on fire while Edmund was sleeping. Quite an uproar in the middle of the night."

"Why ever weren't you using a screen?" scolded his aunt and Edmund felt himself flushing, reluctant to tell her he was so drunk he could remember nothing of the night before. "Well, never mind," she said magnanimously. "You are unhurt, which is all that matters."

"You can thank Samson, here, for that," said Edmund. "I was, er, sleeping soundly. He came to the room and saw the fire and carried me out." Samson sat uncomfortably under the scrutiny of so many pairs of noble eyes, but Edmund seemed not to notice. He beamed proudly on his crony. "By the bye, why did you come to my room?" he asked.

"Fingers Freddy," replied Samson. All the noble eyes continued to stare at him and he shrugged his shoulders nervously inside his jacket. "You was right. I came to tell you."

"Fingers Freddy?" repeated Susan weakly.

"He was hung on July fourteenth," Samson

informed her, as if that explained everything.

"Oh," she said, and attempted a polite smile.

"Didn't I tell you?" crowed Edmund.

Lady Mary deemed it best to change the subject and asked her nephew how he found his new domain.

"Vast," confessed Edmund. "I shan't have a clue how to get on."

"That is not surprising," murmered Jarvis maliciously.

"Sour grapes, Jarvis," reprimanded her ladyship. "Since it galls you so much to stay here and see Edmund restored to his rightful position, I wonder you remain." She turned her gaze on the earl. "You look to be in excellent health, now, Jonathan. When will you be leaving?"

Embarrassed by his aunt's speech, Edmund rushed to speak before his cousin. "There is no hurry for him to leave. We are all rubbing along quite well," he lied.

Samson's eyes grew to twice their size.

"Thank you, Edmund," said the earl. "You have a generous heart and you know what is due your elders."

"Humph," snorted her ladyship. "I can think of a word other than generous which better describes my nephew."

Edmund squirmed. He turned to Susan. "Have you seen the pleasure garden?" he asked.

"Yes," she replied. "But I never tire of walking in it," she added with a smile.

Edmund beamed on her as if she had rescued him from great peril.

Samson looked nervously at the remaining company. "Er, I'll come, too, Dickie boy. I could use a good stretch of the legs." And with that he beat a hasty retreat from the drawing room behind Edmund and Susan.

Once outside, he discreetly discovered a pressing need to visit the stables and check on his horse.

Susan frowned at his retreating back. "Your friend is nervous in our company," she observed.

"He's just not used to nobs," said Edmund.

"He hardly belongs at a house party. Surely you can see that. He is so . . ." Susan paused, searching for a word. "Unpolished," she concluded.

"He has a more noble heart than many of the people I met in London," said Edmund. "Including my fine cousin." He faced Susan, suddenly the teacher and she the pupil. "Sometimes I think you look too much on the outside," he said. She blushed and said nothing. Edmund shrugged. "Ah, well. It is the way you were raised, no doubt. Perhaps I was fortunate to have been spared a noble upbringing."

Susan looked shocked at this. "Edmund!" she exclaimed.

"Samson saved my life, you know," he said.

Susan admitted defeat. "He did," she agreed. "And we must all be grateful to him for doing so. How did it all happen?"

"I don't know," said Edmund. "I wasn't exactly alert. Probably as my cousin says—a spark from the hearth."

Susan shook her head. "Queer, very queer."

"It certainly is," agreed Lady Mary thoughtfully, when Susan later recounted her conversation with Edmund. "It is a good thing we came when we did."

"Aunt, you don't think . . . ?"

Lady Mary nodded. "I am sure of it. First footpads in London. Now a fire. Someone in this family means the new duke harm."

A picture of Jarvis's sneering face sprang to Susan's mind, but she rejected it. Jarvis disliked his cousin intensely, but surely he would never contemplate murder. "You must be mistaken," she said. "Someone of birth would surely never do such a thing."

"My dear child, I am afraid I must disabuse you of some very mistaken notions," said her ladyship. "The Upper Ten Thousand has its fair share of rogues and scoundrels, just as do the lower classes. Naturally, you have been sheltered, and there are many things you don't know. And that is as it should be. But if we are to help Edmund I shall have to ask you to set aside any prejudices that may cloud your vision. I suspected it before. Now I am sure of it. Edmund is in danger. And from someone in this family."

15

THE HOUSE PARTY gathered in the drawing room and waited for the summons to dinner. Jarvis was charming and pleasant to Susan, and respectful to Lady Mary. As usual, he said as little as possible to his host and completely ignored Samson. His father spoke to Edmund with a false jollity which Edmund found jarring and more irritating than his son's coldness to him.

Susan observed Jarvis's cold treatment of his cousin. "I had thought, perhaps, after spending some time in each other's company you and Edmund might have become friends," she said at last.

"Do enemies ever become friends?" countered Jarvis.

"He is your cousin," said Susan gently.

"So I have been told," Jarvis replied.

Susan was spared the necessity of saying anything more as Ames arrived and announced dinner.

After dinner, the ladies repaired to the drawing room and left the gentlemen to their wine. Samson, for whom the meal had been obvious torture, managed to excuse himself before the party regrouped in the drawing room.

"Where is your friend?" asked Lady Mary.

"He went for a walk," replied Edmund.

"Thank heaven," murmured Jarvis.

"The man is plainly nervous in our company," said her ladyship. "You realize, Edmund, that he does not belong."

Edmund's jaw jutted out mulishly. "He is my friend."

"If he is your friend, why not reward him properly?" suggested her ladyship.

"How?" asked Edmund.

"Offer him a position in your employ," she said.

"Smashing idea!" exclaimed Edmund, slapping his thigh. "He can replace Masterson as my valet."

Jarvis burst out laughing at this. "Oh, that is rich," he chortled, ignoring his cousin's angry look. "The gentleman and his gentleman's gentleman."

"Why not give him a job doing something he knows?" suggested Lady Mary.

"Such as robbing your departing guests or your neighbors' coaches," suggested Jarvis.

Edmund jumped from his chair.

"Edmund! Sit down at once," commanded his aunt. "Control yourself. And Jarvis, might I remind you there are ladies present? I will beg you to hold your tongue and stop trying to pick a quarrel with your cousin. Now," she continued as Edmund subsided into his seat. "I was thinking of a job as groom or coachman. Would your friend care for such a thing?"

"Don't I already have a groom and a coachman?" asked Edmund. His cousin smiled sardonically and Edmund cast him an angry glance.

"Well, yes," admitted his aunt. "Of course, you have a coachman."

"Then I can hardly hire Samson and put some other fellow out." Edmund shook his head. "And besides, I need a valet. 'Tis no difficult thing to shave a man."

His aunt politely made no comment on the nicks decorating his chin, mocking testimony as to how simple he had found shaving since the departure of his valet.

Samson was duly hired to replace Masterson that very night, and the following morning reported to his new employer looking extremely self-conscious. "I don't know, Dickie boy. I've never done this man-milliner stuff. I ain't sure 'tis me lay."

"Nonsense," said Edmund heartily. "How hard is it to shave a man? And at least you won't end up being gallows meat if you work for me."

Samson didn't look convinced, but he picked up the razor and prepared to shave his new master, anyway.

"Ow!" yelped Edmund with the first stroke of the blade. "What the devil are you trying to do, cut my bloody neck?"

"Sorry," muttered Samson.

He tried again. Edmund swore and snatched the razor from him. "Never mind. I'll take care of my own bloody shave. See if you can find me a shirt and a cravat."

Samson did his best, but even the combined efforts of the new valet and his master couldn't get Edmund properly turned out. The duke's coat was decorated with lint and his shirt was wrinkled. His cravat was sloppily tied, and his face bore the unattractive marks of Samson's ministrations. Samson frowned at his handiwork and shook his head doubtfully. "I don't know, Dickie boy. I've seen you better turned out when you was dressin' yerself at the Blue Boar. And you've given your own self a better shave, too."

The cuts Edmund had given himself were nearly as fresh as the ones Samson had made. He frowned. Perhaps shaving was one of those things one had to keep one's hand in, like picking pockets. After having had a valet these past months, he'd certainly lost the knack. He shrugged at his reflection. "It will have to do," he said.

Edmund made his appearance at breakfast and was greeted by impolite hooting from his cousin. "If your valet ever tires of working for you send him to me."

"Oh, do stop picking on him," scolded Susan.

Jarvis raised an eyebrow at Edmund. "You have a new champion, cousin?" He smiled on Susan. "If I had but known your tastes ran to more plebeian men, my dear, I should have been less careful with my cravat, perhaps tried my hand at holding up a carriage or two."

"Really, Jarvis," said Susan. "You are acting like a spoilt child whose favorite toy has been taken from him."

Jarvis's smile froze and his eyes narrowed. "You would call a title and an estate—my birthright—toys?"

"They were not rightfully yours," pointed out Susan. "They were Edmund's."

"Yes, Edmund's. Not this imposter's."

"Imposter!" spluttered Edmund.

"That is what I said, sir," replied Jarvis coldly.

Susan laid a hand on Edmund's arm. "Don't listen to him. He is trying to goad you into a quarrel."

Edmund sat back in his chair. "I am an ill-tempered fellow. Forgive me, cousin. I make a poor host. If you will excuse me, I have a meeting with the bailiff this morning." He left them, his breakfast as unfinished as his quarrel with his cousin.

"How do you find your estate?" Susan asked him later that afternoon as they walked in the garden.

Edmund sighed. "Oh, Morton has things well in hand. He seems a trustworthy enough fellow. I am sure he thinks me a great dunderhead." He plopped despondently onto a stone bench.

"Nonsense," said Susan, sitting down next to him. "It is all confusing because it is new to you. I am sure in no time you will feel very much at home."

"I wonder if I shall ever feel at home here," said Edmund. "Dukedom is a very wearing thing."

He looked at Susan and smiled. "It distracts one from the important things of life." He slid an arm around her waist.

"Now, Edmund," she began.

"We have talked enough, don't you think?" he said, bending his head to kiss her.

"Edmund!" Susan put her hand to his lips and he took it and kissed it.

"That will do for a start," he said.

"That will do. Period," Susan informed him.

"Now, Susan. Must we play these little games? We both know you want me to kiss you. Why are you acting like this?"

"It is most improper, and well you know it," she said. "Now, do behave yourself."

"Not proper," grumbled Edmund. "I'm curst tired of being proper. I think I shall take Samson and go nab me some baubles."

"Edmund," Susan reproved. "Shame on you." Edmund frowned and she studied him. "You are only behaving this way because you have allowed your cousin to nettle you."

"If Jarvis were Grayborough would you marry him?" asked Edmund suddenly.

"Of course not!" declared Susan.

"He is much better suited to be a duke than I. And he will, most likely, make a far better husband as well."

"Your cousin is proud and selfish," said Susan. "I shouldn't have him on a platter."

Edmund turned to her, a slow smile creeping across his face. "Why did you accompany my aunt here?" he asked.

Susan blushed. "She wished me to come," she stammered.

Edmund's mouth was hovering near her shoulder. "And that is the only reason?" he asked.

Susan stood up. "Perhaps we should go into the house," she suggested.

Edmund rose and followed her, a smile of triumph on his lips. As soon as he got rid of his pesky cousins he would bring out that little package from Rundell and Bridge, make his marriage proposal, and have his kiss.

While Edmund and Susan had been walking in the pleasure garden, Lady Mary and the earl had been conversing in the library. "Of course there was a fire in Edmund's hearth that night!" the earl was exclaiming.

"At this time of year? How very odd that none of the servants wish to claim responsibility for starting one," said her ladyship.

"Of course not. No one wishes to be blamed for carelessness. What bug have you got in your bonnet, Mary?"

"Edmund has had some very dangerous accidents since he stepped into your shoes, Jonathan. Odd, is it not?"

The earl's face turned a dark red. "What are you implying?"

"I think we both know. Take Jarvis and return to Weatherwelle. It is time you admitted defeat."

The earl made no reply, but stalked from the room.

That night he revealed his intention to return to his own estate. "I am feeling much better and it is time we went home and attended to our own affairs," he concluded.

"As you wish," said Edmund politely. "I am sure you know you are most welcome any time you wish to visit."

"How very gracious," murmured Jarvis.

"I am trying," retorted Edmund. "Though, God knows, there have been those who have done their best to make it difficult."

Jarvis made no reply, but took a sip of wine.

The following morning, as the unwanted house-guests were making preparations to depart, Edmund was trying to submit to the ministrations of his valet. "Ouch! Watch it, man. You want to slit my gullet?" he complained.

"Sorry," mumbled Samson. Silence fell between the friends, and, for a few moments, all that could be heard was the soft scrape of blade on flesh. "You know, Dickie boy," said Samson at last. "I don't know as I like all this valet business. Having to put up with that stiff butler of yours is nearly as bad as elbowing it with the nobs."

"You want a different position?" asked Edmund.

Samson shook his head slowly. "No. What I really want is . . ." He paused.

"Out with it, man. What?"

"I always fancied meself as an ale draper. I want a little tavern. Like the Blue Boar. In fact, 'tis the Blue Boar I want."

"The Blue Boar? Is old Jonsey thinking of selling, then?"

Samson nodded. "His daughter married a cit. Wants him and the missus to come live with her."

Edmund thought for a moment. "Damn if I won't set you up, old fellow! 'Tis the least I can do for you after you saved my life, and that not for the first time."

"Aye," said Samson cheerfully. "We had some adventures, didn't we, Dickie boy?"

"Yes. But you are getting too old for such doings. You should be settling down with Mary to raise yourself a pack of ruffians." Samson grinned foolishly at this and Edmund gave him a playful shove. "Here. Hand over the razor. As you are no longer in my employ I think I shall do better to shave my own self."

After much hustle and bustle, the cousins were seen safely packed into their carriage. The earl had been as hearty in his thanks as his son had been cool. Edmund had been glad to be rid of both, and in his relief his farewell was nearly as hearty as the former duke's. He turned back inside the house with his aunt and Susan, and fairly skipped into the drawing room. "I feel as if ten sacks of grain have been lifted from my shoulders," he said.

"And so you should," said his aunt. "Enjoy your freedom while it lasts."

"What might you mean by that?" asked Edmund.

"Only that you have not seen the last of them. You left the door wide open last night and Jonathan will be coming back in it before the cat's had time to lick her ear. Mark my words."

Edmund frowned. "That is a fine way to spoil a fellow's morning, I must say."

"You should have told them you wished to see no more of them here," said Lady Mary. "I am sure your cousins will want to come visit you this autumn. Of course, they have pheasants enough to shoot on their own land, but they will insist on coming to see you, nonetheless, for coming to Grayborough Hall for a little shooting will make a convenient excuse to reestablish themselves here."

"Ah, well. I suppose I can stomach 'em for a while this autumn now that they are gone for the rest of the summer," said Edmund cheerfully.

"I shall want to be a part of that house party," said her ladyship, "so please write and inform me when you hear from Jonathan."

"Since when have you become so fond of our cousins' company?" wondered Edmund.

"Never you mind," said his aunt. "Only promise to write me. And Edmund."

"Yes?"

"Find yourself a valet."

16

ONCE THE RESTRAINING company of his relatives was gone, Edmund wasted little time. "There is a boat down by the stream," he told Susan. "Would you care to take a basket of food and see the world from a fish's view this afternoon?"

Susan consented, and armed with enough food for five people they set out to try their hand at boating.

They arrived at the stream and Edmund tossed his coat on the bank, pulled off his boots, and set to work launching the skiff.

He was able to get the boat in the water without incident. And he succeeded in handing in both Susan and the picnic basket. Getting himself in, however, proved to be a more difficult matter. For a moment, he stood, one foot in the bow and one on the bank, wobbling to get his balance and bring the other leg inside. "Do be careful," cautioned Susan.

The boat did not wait for Edmund to make up his mind. It bobbed further from shore, splitting Edmund's legs until he finally splashed into the water. He hauled himself inside, almost tipping them. Susan stopped giggling and grabbed both sides of the rocking boat, trying to steady it. The boat subsided and her giggles returned.

"It would appear that, like so much of my previous life, I have forgotten how to launch a boat," admitted Edmund sheepishly.

Susan was now all concern. "We should go back. You will want dry clothes."

"Bah," scoffed Edmund. "On a hot day such as this? I shall dry in no time." He began to unbutton his wet shirt.

And as he did so a mottled red began to climb Susan's neck. She looked away.

Edmund tossed the sodden shirt aside. "That's better," he sighed happily, then noticed his companion was not looking at him. He also noted the deep blush on her cheeks and frowned. "Are you going to be this missish all afternoon?" he inquired.

Susan looked insulted. "I am not being missish," she said. "It is just that being here with you without your shirt on is so . . ."

"Improper," Edmund finished with her. "Well, then, perhaps you would care to eat your cold chicken looking at the trees on the bank," he said nonchalantly. "And while you are getting something for yourself, please open the basket and pass me a leg."

Susan was highly displeased by such callous

disregard for her feelings. Frowning and still averting her gaze from the offending chest, she took the covering napkin from the basket. Her eyes grew wide.

"Open it," suggested Edmund, smiling.

Susan picked up the long, narrow box. She opened it and gasped. Inside lay an emerald necklace and matching emerald drops for her ears. She looked up, blushing again.

Edmund smiled at her. "I love you with all my heart. Won't you please say yes this time?"

Tears sprung to Susan's eyes. "Oh, Edmund."

"You will marry me?" he asked eagerly.

"Yes. Oh, yes!"

"Yes! She said yes!" Edmund jumped up in delight and the inevitable happened. The boat tilted them into the water. They came up spluttering and laughing. Susan pushed a sodden lock from her face and smiled. "Such a proposal. I never thought I should become betrothed chest deep in water." A look of sudden horror came on her face. "The jewels!" she gasped. "They must have flown from my hand when I fell in. Oh, gracious!"

Edmund disappeared, diving under the water. Within a moment he was back, the box in his hand. He gave it to her and she hugged it, smiling lovingly up at him.

There she stood, eyes shining, face gleaming with water, limp locks framing her face. Edmund had never seen a more beautiful sight. He embraced his love and kissed her, causing her to lose her footing and himself to lose his balance, and they went under again.

Once more they came up coughing. "We will both drown this way," he said, and scooped her up and carried her back to shore.

If Edmund had thought his love looked beautiful chest deep in a quiet stream, he found she was now nothing less than ravishing on the bank. Her sodden gown clung to her, revealing every delicious line and curve of her body. Edmund pulled her to him and kissed her, and for the first time in her life, Miss Susan Montague experienced a passionate kiss from an experienced man.

"Oh, Edmund," she sighed, when he finally reluctantly released her.

"I may disappoint you as a sailor," he murmured. "But I promise you, I shan't disappoint you as a lover." Susan's face turned a deep red at this and he chuckled and picked up his coat, draping it over her shoulders. "Wait here and I shall swim out and rescue the boat."

They walked back to the Hall hand in hand, and it wasn't difficult for Lady Mary, who saw them coming from the window, to discern what had occurred. She smiled. " 'Tis about time," she said.

Of course, later that afternoon when the happy couple cornered her in the library, she feigned surprise. She didn't need to feign delight. "For truly, I have hoped from the start this would happen," she said. "I am sure you will both be very happy."

"When shall we marry? Next month?" suggested Edmund.

Both ladies looked at him as if he were mad. "We must have time to plan the wedding," said Susan.

"And then there are the bride clothes to be made, and the trousseau," put in Lady Mary. "The church must be reserved."

"All the relatives written. . . ."

Edmund moaned. "How long will that take?"

"A June wedding is quite nice," suggested Susan.

"June!" exclaimed Edmund in horror.

"April?"

Edmund was still frowning.

"When would you prefer?" asked Susan.

"Next month," he replied.

"Edmund, do be reasonable," his aunt remonstrated.

"Very well. Let us compromise. What do you say to a December wedding? What better way to ring in the holidays? And we can be married here at the Hall if you like."

"But the weather is often so bad," protested Susan.

Edmund sighed.

"It is not so very long till April," said Susan.

"Oh, very well," he said. "April it is."

"Good. Then, that is settled," said his aunt. She turned to Susan. "I think we should leave at the end of the week."

"Leave! But you have only just gotten here," protested Edmund.

"There is much to be done, and Susan's mother will want to know of your betrothal."

"We can send her a letter," he suggested.

Again, both ladies looked at him, this time as though he was dull-witted. "Edmund, really. You should certainly have enough to occupy you until we return this autumn."

"And you may come and spend the Christmas holidays with my family," put in Susan.

"Meanwhile," said Lady Mary, "you will still have your friend here to bear you company."

"No, I won't," said Edmund. "I shall be all alone," he finished pitifully.

"Where is your friend going?" asked his aunt.

"Back to the Blue Boar. He is going to purchase it and settle down."

His aunt sighed. "Pity," she said. Then, bracingly, "Well, you will be busy enough, learning about the estate, getting acquainted with your tenants. You will still have plenty to occupy yourself."

"Nothing occupies me as pleasantly as Susan," Edmund said, and she smiled and put her hand on his. "Will you bring your family when you return?" he asked.

"Do you ask in invitation or out of concern?" she replied.

"I should like to meet your family," insisted Edmund. "We will have a big celebration when they come. A ball, perhaps, or a dinner?"

His aunt chuckled and shook her head. "You will not live a quiet life with our Edmund, my dear."

Susan lowered her eyes. "I will not mind what kind of life I live, so long as it is with Edmund," she said shyly and Edmund squeezed her hand.

The remainder of the week went much too fast for Edmund's tastes. He and Susan tried to fill it as much as possible with long walks and quiet tête-à-têtes in the drawing room after his aunt had retired for the evening, but it seemed they couldn't get enough of each other's company, and the morning his guests were due to leave, he awoke feeling glum.

Even as the imminent departure of his last houseguests hung over him, however, a new arrival appeared. John Snow was his name. He was a valet and came bearing a letter from Edmund's cousin. "Father and I both feel your friend is not suited to the role of gentleman's gentleman, and will be happier in another position in your employ. So I send you Mr. John Snow. I understand he is highly skilled with a cravat. Our best wishes to you and sincerest thanks for the hospitality we enjoyed at Grayborough Hall. Yours, etc."

So, here was an olive branch from his cousins in the person of Mr. Snow. Edmund shrugged mentally. Why not? "Well, Mr. Snow. As you can see, I am very much in need of a valet. Your services will be appreciated." He rang the bellpull. "I'll have Ames show you to your room, then go fetch yourself some breakfast. I shan't need you till . . ." Edmund stopped. By dinner there would be no one in the great house but himself. No sense dressing, then. Who was there to dress for? "Tomorrow morning," he finished. "Spend the day looking about the place."

"Your Grace won't wish to dress for dinner?"

"No," said His Grace glumly.

The butler escorted the new valet from the room unnoticed. The only departure Edmund was seeing was Susan's. "April," he muttered. Ah, well, he tried to console himself, the ladies would be back, and bringing Susan's family, too, in only a few weeks. On that pleasant thought, he went in search of breakfast.

Lady Mary and Susan were already in the dining room. "We thought, perhaps, you were still sleeping," said his aunt.

"I would certainly not sleep away my last precious hour with my two favorite ladies," he said, smiling, and bent to kiss his aunt's cheek.

"Rogue," she said. "I know well with whom you wish to spend your last precious hour, and it isn't myself."

Edmund winked at Susan and went to the sideboard to fill his plate. "I had a visitor before breakfast, and you will be happy to know, Aunt, that I now have a new valet."

"No!" exclaimed his aunt in disbelief.

Edmund nodded. "The Wortleys have sent him. I think, perhaps, they wish to mend fences."

Lady Mary looked skeptical. "They wish to feather their own nest, you mean." She laid down her fork. "I wish your friend had stayed a little longer."

"Samson? You yourself told me he didn't belong."

"Not in the drawing room, certainly. But I thought you might find him a position somewhere on the estate."

Edmund shook his head. "He didn't fancy one. He wants to get spliced." The two women looked at him blankly. "Married," he explained. "Yes, 'tis a happy ending for a couple of old snafflers."

Lady Mary gave Edmund a reprimanding look. "I think we have heard quite enough cant this morning," she informed him.

"Sorry," he said humbly, and dug into his eggs.

Breakfast ended much too quickly, and Edmund soon found himself waving good-bye to his aunt and a teary-eyed Susan. He reentered the great house with reluctance. It seemed not to want him, and he left it to spend the rest of the day moping on the bank of the stream where he had finally won his Susan.

Edmund's temperament being what it was, it was impossible for him to remain melancholy for long. He awoke the next day optimistic that time would pass swiftly and Susan as well as her family would soon be with him. Meanwhile, he would throw himself into learning about his estate. He would ride out every day, and by fall he would know all his tenants. He would know everything there was to know about cows and sheep and crops. Ha! That would be one in the peepers for his cousin Jarvis.

In this pleasant frame of mind, Edmund received his new valet. He smiled on John Snow, prepared to be pleased with the fellow's ministrations. Anyone would be better than the priggish Masterson. And anything had to be better than the handiwork of Samson.

Mr. Snow prepared to shave his master. He took his time sharpening the razor and Edmund admired his thoroughness. Snow smiled calmly at his master as he laid a warm, wet towel over his face.

" 'Tis nice to have a fellow who knows his business," said Edmund's muffled voice from under the towel. "My last valet nearly slit my gullet."

Mr. Snow removed the towel and lathered his master's chin and neck. "Shaving is an art," he said, and took Edmund's face firmly in his hand.

So firmly, in fact, that Edmund found himself feeling suddenly uneasy. He tried to pull his head away from the grasp, but the hand only tightened. "If Your Grace could hold a little more still . . ."

 **17**

EDMUND FELT THE blade dig into his throat and sent an elbow into the man's midsection. It took Snow by surprise and he doubled over. Edmund grabbed the towel and put it to his bleeding throat.

The valet stood with both arms wrapped around his wounded middle, gasping for breath. The look on his face was one of fear. Fear of what? Fear of his master's wrath? Or fear of something else, such as being caught? Had the cove been trying to slit his throat?

"Your Grace, you must sit still," said Mr. Snow at last. "You very nearly made me have a terrible accident."

Edmund had not lived the life he lived for nothing. His eyes narrowed. "That was no accident, I'll wager. You'd better turn stag, for the game is up." The man stood gaping at him, and Edmund grabbed him by the coat. "Tell me who put you up to this," he growled.

"Really, Your Grace. I have no idea what you are talking about," protested Snow, eyes wide. Edmund threw the man from him. These men-milliners were all alike, hiding behind the manners of the nobs. "Take the references you came with and go find yourself another position."

The man made no protest. He hurried from the room as if thankful to be in one piece.

Edmund examined his cut in his looking glass. It was a nasty nick. Had it been an accident or had cousin Jarvis bribed this John Snow to do away with his inconvenient cousin? Edmund found himself suddenly disinclined to see the Wortleys come fall.

But as a lonely August dawdled by, he began to think even their presence would be preferable to only the company of servants, and the letter announcing their intended visit was very nearly a welcome one. At any rate it would bring Susan back, he thought cheerfully, as well as his aunt. And Susan's family. Edmund rubbed his hands together gleefully. The old house would be humming then! He wrote to his aunt immediately.

The Wortleys were the first to arrive and Edmund welcomed them graciously, if not warmly. His cousins, it seemed, were determined to let bygones be bygones. The earl was effusive in greeting Edmund, and his cousin Jarvis was, at least, polite.

He left them to their own devices until dinner, as much for his own sake as theirs. What the devil did one say to such a pair of rotten slyboots, anyway—"Surprised to see me alive?" Or, "Hired any murderers lately?" Of course, it was possible that the fellow, Snow, hadn't meant to do him in at all.

Dinner went smoothly enough. The former duke allowed no awkward silences, waxing eloquent on everything from the days when Edmund's father was alive to the joys of shooting pheasant.

"How did your valet work out?" asked Jarvis after the servants had withdrawn and the three men settled in with their after-dinner wine.

What was this, incredible cheek or innocence? "He didn't," replied Edmund. "The fellow had a most unsteady hand. I turned him out."

"Pity," said Jarvis. "He was highly recommended."

As what? wondered Edmund cynically, but he kept his peace.

"So you are, once again, acting as your own valet?" asked Jarvis.

A simple question coming from anyone else. Edmund's eyes narrowed, but he got ahold of himself and shrugged nonchalantly. "How long did you say you will be staying?" he asked the earl.

Jarvis smiled. "My cousin learns fast," he murmured and took a sip of wine.

The former duke had been evasive in his answer. Edmund went to bed with a sinking feeling that he would be stuck with his unwanted relatives until the end of the world.

But his spirits rose considerably when, the next day, his aunt and Susan arrived. The passionate hug with which Edmund greeted Susan was not lost on Jarvis and he raised a questioning eyebrow at her. She chose to ignore him, concentrating instead on explaining to Edmund why her mother and sisters had not come along. "Bella has contracted the mumps, and Mama is worried Annie, too, will catch them. She didn't dare leave them and thought it best to wait and come all together when she is sure everyone is well. I am sure they will be with us by the end of the month."

"They will be welcome as soon as they are able to come," said Edmund.

"You didn't tell us there were to be other members of this house party, dear boy," said the earl as the ladies went to their rooms to freshen and change.

Edmund felt a guilty warmth on his cheeks. "They wished to join us," he said.

Dinner that evening was a relatively gay affair. Jarvis managed to restrain himself from any barbed comments. His father was, once more, uncharacteristically jovial. Even Lady Mary refrained from caustic remarks, and Susan—Susan, thought Edmund, looked exceptionally ravishing this night in a dark green gown, the emerald necklace glittering on her long neck, the emerald drops swinging from her ears. Who could misbehave in her presence? He beamed at her.

"I wonder," said Jarvis, observing his cousin. "Will we be reading an announcement in the *Gazette* soon?"

"Never mind town gossip," huffed his father. "What I want to know is, what time will we be going out after some birds tomorrow?"

"It will most likely rain tomorrow," said Lady Mary. "I suggest you wait."

"A little damp won't hurt us," said Jarvis, and sneezed.

"There," said her ladyship. "You are coming down with a cold. If you go out in the damp all day you are bound to return with a putrid sore throat. And Jonathan, after your illness last spring a cold could be disastrous. I would advise you not to go."

"I thank you for your advice, Mary," said the earl. "But as you are not my doctor, I am sure it won't offend you if I don't take it."

"I don't see why you all cannot wait a day or two," insisted Lady Mary.

"I am looking forward to going out," said Edmund diplomatically. "What time shall we leave?"

Lady Mary scowled as the men made their plans, but said nothing more.

Dessert was consumed, and the ladies departed to await the gentlemen in the drawing room. "What is wrong?" asked Susan. "Why did you try to discourage that hunting party?"

"I have a bad feeling about it," replied her ladyship. " 'Tis nothing I can prove. I only know there will be three men in the woods tomorrow with guns. One of them is Grayborough. The second is a careless old fool. And the third is a bitter young man who feels himself deprived of his inheritance and knows the story of the accidental death of the Grayborough heir."

Susan bit her lip.

"'Tis only a presentiment. But remember, since he became duke our Edmund has been set upon by footpads, then nearly burned in his room. This could . . . Hush. Here they come." Lady Mary smiled at the gentlemen. "Well. I must say you did not linger long over your wine," she said.

"With two lovely ladies awaiting us? Never," said Jarvis.

Susan looked at Edmund desperately. "It is a lovely night for a walk in the garden," she said.

"So it is," he agreed, smiling.

"I'll just get my shawl," she told him, and hurried off.

"So the new duke wins the lovely Miss Montague as well as the title," observed Jarvis.

Edmund heard the bitter tinge in his cousin's voice and felt suddenly uncomfortable with his good fortune. He could think of nothing to say, and so stood mutely and let the conversation flow around him. Surely he must be the luckiest man alive, and the most undeserving. His cousin obviously thought him so.

Susan returned and he escorted her out into the garden. Once in the garden, Edmund discovered her thoughts had not been of kisses and sweet confessions of love. "Please do not go out shooting tomorrow with your cousins," she begged.

"What's this? You want to waste our time together worrying about dampness and colds?"

"'Tis more than a cold that threatens you," said Susan. "Your aunt is sure you are in danger and I am, too."

"Nonsense," scoffed Edmund.

"Oh, Edmund. As you value your life, as you value our love, please do not go out tomorrow. I know you are in danger. I can feel it around us, like some great beast waiting to devour our happiness."

"Nothing is going to devour our happiness," said Edmund firmly. "And speaking of devouring, I have been waiting all day to taste those sweet lips."

But Susan's lips were not sweet. They were salty. "I am afraid," she sobbed. "Please don't go."

"Here now. A petty, white-livered fellow I should look if I backed out."

"Please, Edmund. For me."

There was nothing Edmund wouldn't do for this woman, except look a coward. "I cannot," he said.

She looked at him as if he had betrayed her and fled the garden in tears.

Edmund watched her go and sighed. He walked back to the house, cursing his cousins for returning to make his new life such a misery.

"Where is Susan?" asked his aunt.

"Headache," improvised Edmund.

Twenty minutes later, while Edmund labored to entertain his guests, a small figure stole from the Hall to the stable, and in less than five minutes had emerged astride a large, snorting bay. The rider kept to a walk until safely down the drive, then let the animal have its head, and galloped off down the road.

Later that night there was a soft knock at Edmund's bedroom door. He grinned. So, the minx had come to collect a kiss and apologize for her earlier behavior. He opened the door, all smiles. "Aunt!"

His aunt stepped into the room. "I cannot like this," she said without preamble. "I have a very bad feeling about it."

"So I have heard," said her nephew.

"I am sure harm will come to you. I have such a strong presentiment that history means to repeat itself."

Edmund blanched. "I have no brother left to shoot," he said.

"There is still an heir and a next in line for the title going out shooting," said his aunt.

Edmund's mouth set in a stubborn line. "I shall be fine," he said. His aunt's face seemed to crumble and she aged years before his eyes. "I shall be careful, love," he said.

"I cannot bear to lose you a second time," she said. Her sentence ended on a sob and she got hold of herself with great effort. "I can see there is nothing I can do to stop you. You are a very foolish, headstrong boy."

Edmund smiled at this. "I am," he agreed, and walked her to the door. "Goodnight, dearest. Pleasant dreams."

"Unpleasant nightmares, more like," she said, and left him.

Edmund slept poorly that night, his own suspicions combining with his aunt's to torment him. As a consequence he overslept the following morning. He arrived for breakfast at ten and found his uncle and cousin both dressed and ready for a day of tramping in the underbrush. Edmund apologized for keeping them waiting. "I overslept," he said. "You should have gone on without me."

"Wouldn't think of it," said the earl. "Hurry and down some victuals, boy, and we'll get started."

Edmund had no desire to hurry. He had no desire to go. He had awakened to see a drizzling mist framed in his bedroom window and did not relish tramping around in the damp with his dislikable cousins. His aunt's words came haunting him: "There is still an heir going out shooting." He shook them off and speared a slice of ham for his plate. "Where is Susan?" he asked his aunt, who sat nursing a cup of tea.

"Still abed, I suppose," replied Her Ladyship. "We have not yet seen her this morning."

Edmund tried not to feel disappointed. Seeing Susan before he left would have gone a long way toward making this day bearable. Well, there was no help for it. He gobbled the rest of his meal and went in search of a warm coat and a gun.

Lady Mary kept the other two men company, sipping tea as if she had not a care in the world. As soon as they had borne Edmund off, however, her face sagged with worry. She suddenly felt very old and unequal to the task of taking care of her nephew. Slowly, as if clawing her way through quicksand, she climbed the stairs and went down the hallway to Susan's bedroom. She tapped on the door. "Susan," she called. There was no answer. She knocked more loudly. "Susan!" Lady Mary opened the door and looked inside. Susan's bed lay unoccupied and pristinely undisturbed. "Dear God. What is this?" cried her ladyship.

None of the household servants seemed to know the whereabouts of Miss Montague, and in the midst of questioning, a new arrival showed. "There is a man looking for his grace," announced the butler, "who claims to have been His Grace's valet. He would like to speak with His Grace and wants to know if he can wait in the kitchen for his return."

James! Her James. The man who Edmund trained to be a fighter. The timing was providential. "Show him in to me immediately," said her ladyship.

They had been out less than an hour and already Edmund was longing to be lounging about his warm house. The drizzling mist had turned to a chilling rain. He had shot a couple of birds, and when last he'd seen the earl the old fellow had gotten one as well. Edmund wondered how many they would have to shoot before they could admit defeat to the weather and go in.

He was as tired of his own company as he was the rain. He had always thought hunting to be a sociable affair, but the earl had left them early on and now Jarvis, too, had drifted away. Edmund had half a mind to turn back and let his cousins continue their tromping through the woods alone. Most likely, they'd never miss him.

He had just come to a decision to go back when he caught sight of a figure deeper in the woods. Now he'd have to stay and be sociable. He waved at the figure and began to walk toward it. He was within twenty feet of the other man when the man raised his gun and pointed it at Edmund.

18

EDMUND STARED AT the figure with the gun. A succession of scenes came spinning through his mind at a dizzying pace. A man raising a gun to his shoulder and shooting a young boy, the boy falling to the ground. Now, here was another boy. The man was turning his rifle on him. The boy was running . . . sobbing. "No!" cried Edmund, clapping his hands to his head and sinking to his knees.

As if on cue, another player ran out from among the trees. "Father!" gasped Jarvis. "What are you doing?"

"Shut up, boy. I'm doing this for you. Do you think I'll have us eased out of the title by a common thief and a fool to boot?"

The subject of this conversation was unable to add anything to it. The shadowy past had at last taken real and vivid form, and the shock had left him insensate on the ground.

"He's had a fool's luck, too," continued the earl. "Couldn't kill him with footpads or with that fire I set. But this time his common friend isn't here to save his worthless hide."

The earl raised his gun. "Father, no!" cried Jarvis, jumping to grab the gun.

"Your Grace!" called a voice somewhere out of sight.

"Leave go, boy!" snapped the earl. "There's no time to waste." With an amazing show of strength, he managed to push his son away. Taken off balance, Jarvis fell. "No!" he cried, trying to get to his feet as his father took aim at the fallen duke.

The muffled sound of hoofbeats in the distance had been growing steadily louder, an underlying rhythm to accompany the drama taking place in the woods. Now they sounded as a nearby crashing in the woods. A huge, black horse burst into sight, ridden by a large, angry-looking man. The horse rushed the earl and the man jumped off, bringing them both to the ground. The gun went off in midair.

"Father!" Jarvis joined the fray.

"Your Grace! Your Grace!" The disembodied voice was nearer now, frantic.

"Edmund!" Susan rode up, jumped from her horse, and ran to her fallen love. She scooped him into her arms as if to protect him from the battling men.

"Your Grace!" James appeared on the scene, fists ready, but unsure as to whom to hit. He settled for rushing into the fray and, catching the big man by surprise, knocked him on the jaw, sending him sprawling on his back, stunned.

"Oh, no!" cried Susan. "Not him. The other!"

Which other? James took a guess and a swing at Jarvis. "Not me, fool," he snapped. James prepared to drop the former duke. "And not him, either." Jarvis picked up his father's gun. "The fighting is at an end." He walked to where Edmund sat, quiet tears rushing down his cheeks as he mourned the return of his memory and the loss of his childhood and his brother. "I . . ." Jarvis was unable to go on. He put a hand on his cousin's shoulder and walked from the woods.

"Your Grace, are you quite all right?" enquired James, rushing to help Edmund to his feet.

Edmund nodded, unable to speak.

James and Susan escorted him back to the house, one on either side, followed by Samson, with both the earl and the horses in tow. By the time they arrived his aunt was standing in the doorway. She scanned her nephew's haggard face. "Edmund," she said. He could only stare mutely at her. "Take him into the drawing room and set him by the fire," she commanded Susan.

The party trooped by her into the drawing room. To Samson she said, "I owe you a great debt, young man. Now I think I know where my niece has been."

The large man nodded. "More'n fourteen hours' hard riding. She's got bottom, that one." He followed the others into the drawing room, leaving the earl to face Lady Mary.

"Your son is packing your things," she said. " 'Tis a pity they took your gun from you. You would have done us all a great service by turning it on yourself." The earl's only reply was to glare at her, and she left him.

In the drawing room Susan had served brandy to all the men. Edmund was in a chair by the fire, staring into the flame. Samson and James stood in nervous silence, trying politely to find something on which to focus their eyes besides their stricken friend.

Her Ladyship knelt at his feet and took his hands in hers. "Edmund, dear," she said softly.

"It was him. He killed my brother. I . . ." He buried his face in his hands and sobbed.

Her ladyship sat next to him and put her arms around him. "There, now. 'Tis over at last," she crooned.

It took another hour and another glass of brandy for Edmund to pull himself together. He smiled wanly at the others. "Sorry to have been making such a cake of myself." Susan came to stand next to him. He smiled at her and pulled her to him. "I guess you and my aunt were right," he said. "I shouldn't have gone out shooting. Samson, old fellow. And James, too?" He looked to where his servant and friend sat perched on the sofa, both looking uncomfortable and out of place. "I can hardly credit it. I thought you were well launched as a prizefighter."

James blushed. "I found it wasn't the life for me. Which is why I am here. I thought, perhaps, Your Grace might be in need of a valet. Or a footman, perhaps?"

"Thank God," murmured her ladyship.

Edmund chuckled. "James, old man, remind me to tell you of what I have been through since I lost you to the ring. And you, giant. What lures you from the Blue Boar?"

"The mort came to me and told me you was goin' to get popped," said Samson. "We rode straight through the night. Didn't get here any too soon, from the looks of it."

Edmund turned to Susan in amazement. "You rode all night, alone?"

"We had to have help," she said. "I felt sure Aunt was right, and I was so afraid for you. It was all I could think to do."

Edmund was overcome once more. Blinking back tears he hugged Susan and buried his face in the fragrant chestnut locks. "However did such a fellow as I find such a jewel?"

Jarvis entered the drawing room, obviously ill at ease. "We are packed and ready to leave," he announced.

Edmund nodded.

Jarvis hesitated. His face seemed to Edmund to be carved from stone. He licked his lower lip and spoke. "Cousin, I have been less than kind. And I must admit, it was largely due to the fact that I never believed your claim. When I remember how we used to play as children . . ." He fell silent, unable to continue.

"Water under the bridge," mumbled Edmund, embarrassed. "Now," he said briskly, "we must deal with the future. What are we going to do with your father?"

"I could take him to the continent, but he would be miserable."

"Then by all means, take him," said Lady Mary.

"You could also take him back to your estate and keep him there," suggested Edmund.

"That would make him nearly as miserable as living on the continent," admitted Jarvis. "Any banishment from Grayborough Hall will be torment for him."

"Then 'tis settled," said Edmund, some of his old heartiness returning. "By the way, cousin. That valet you sent to me. He wasn't, perchance, anyone your father recommended, was he?"

Jarvis shook his head. "No. Snow was valet to an acquaintance. The man had had the misfortune to break his neck in a curricle accident and Snow was in need of a position." Jarvis shrugged. "I thought, perhaps, you could use him."

"Blast!" muttered Edmund. "And I thought he meant to cut my throat."

Jarvis smiled sadly. "Who could blame you for thinking such a thing?" He turned to go.

"Jarvis," called Edmund.

Jarvis stopped.

"I hope simply because your father is no longer welcome here that you will not make yourself a stranger."

For a moment strong emotion prevented Jarvis from speaking. "Thank you," he said at last and strode quickly from the room.

Lady Mary's eyes misted. "You are a good man," she said. "You will do honor to the title. More than that scoundrel, Jonathan, ever could have."

She shook her head. "Somehow, it never occurred to me that your brother's death could have been other than what Jonathan said it was: an accidental shooting, with you pulling the trigger. I thought I was the only one looking for you all these years, but it wouldn't surprise me to learn that he had hired searchers as well. How different our motives in wishing to find you!"

"So you weren't worrying about Jonathan trying to kill me," said Edmund.

Lady Mary shook her head. "All along I thought it was Jarvis."

"Did you think it was Jarvis?" Edmund asked Susan, but on looking down at her, discovered she was fast asleep on his shoulder. "If you will excuse me," he said, lifting her from the chair. "I think I shall escort Miss Montague to her room."

He carried Susan upstairs and laid her gently on her bed. She stirred. "Sweet dreams, sweetheart," he whispered.

"Edmund," she murmured.

"Yes, love."

"I think a Christmas wedding would be lovely." With that she sighed and rolled on her side.

Edmund smiled and kissed her forehead. He left Susan and, instead of rejoining the others in the drawing room, went outside. The Duke of Grayborough walked down the tree-lined drive, then turned to look at his childhood home. Grayborough Hall beamed brightly in the afternoon sunlight—nearly as brightly as his future.